W9-CJN-719

J. T. EDSON'S
FLOATING OUTFIT

The toughest bunch of Rebels that ever lost a war, they fought for the South, and then for Texas, as the legendary Floating Outfit of "Ole Devil" Hardin's O.D. Connected ranch.

MARK COUNTER was the best-dressed man in the West: always dressed fit-to-kill. **BELLE BOYD** was as deadly as she was beautiful, with a "Manhattan" model Colt tucked under her long skirts. **THE YSABEL KID** was Comanche fast and Texas tough. And the most famous of them all was **DUSTY FOG**, the ex-cavalryman known as the Rio Hondo Gun Wizard.

J. T. Edson has captured all the excitement and adventure of the raw frontier in this magnificent Western series. Turn the page for a complete list of Berkley Floating Outfit titles.

J.T. Edson

WAGONS TO BACKSIGHT

BERKLEY BOOKS, NEW YORK

text of the original edition.
It has been completely reset in a typeface
designed for easy reading, and was printed
from new film.

WAGONS TO BACKSIGHT

A Berkley Book / published by arrangement with
Transworld Publishers, Ltd.

PRINTING HISTORY
Originally published in Great Britain, by Brown Watson Limited.
Corgi edition published 1969
Berkley edition / December 1980
Second printing / December 1982

ISBN: 0-425-05951-0

A BERKLEY BOOK ® TM 757,375
Berkley Books are published by Berkley Publishing Corporation,
200 Madison Avenue, New York, New York 10016.
The name ''BERKLEY'' and the stylized ''B'' with design
are trademarks belonging to Berkley Publishing Corporation.
PRINTED IN THE UNITED STATES OF AMERICA

For "Rocky" Byford, having known him twenty years without learning his first name!

CHAPTER ONE

Tom Blade Puts Down His Roots

THE two riders about a mile ahead of the wagon train formed something of a contrast, although both were excellent horsemen. Tall, slim, distinguished looking, Colonel Raines wore a white Confederate campaign hat, clean buckskin jacket, white shirt with gray trousers tucked into shining riding boots and carried an Army Colt in a closed-top holster. On the other hand, Tom Blade rode slouched in his saddle, unlike the Colonel's erect cavalry seat, had on a black Stetson, smoke-darkened buckskins and moccasins.

"How do you like us, Tom?" asked Raines.

A twinkle came to Blade's sun-squinted eyes. "Passing fine, Colonel. I've made six trips west since the War and this's been the best. Mind, the other times I had Yankees along."

Raines smiled. This train might be Confederate but owed its existence to the aid of a Yankee. General Mansfield, Governor of Arizona Territory, wore the blue in the War, yet he did not forget his old West Point classmate when Raines wrote for a suggestion of a new home. The reply came quickly. Up near the Grand Canyon lay a small hamlet called Backsight in the heart of cattle country and sorely in need of a township of some size to take its place. So Raines gathered people around him, hired Tom Blade as scout and headed west. The wagons carried a six months' stock of supplies for resale and home consumption as the travelers intended to run businesses rather than ranch or farm. They needed to be self-supporting until such time as a wagon route would be established to one of the larger towns.

"Have you thought over what we discussed yesterday, Tom?"

"Thought some about it, Colonel. I've never settled down any place since the War. Never took to anybody enough to want to settle."

"A man should put down roots, Tom," Raines replied. "I know you'd like to go back to the Rio Hondo but there's a place for you. We need someone just like you to handle the law. There's that other trouble too."

Tom Blade nodded. Over the head of Colonel Raines and the train hung a threat which only the two men and Raines' daughter, Louise, knew about. It hung over them, hovering unseen yet always there, just waiting for a chance to strike.

"I've thought some about that, too," replied Blade. "Been thinking about it ever since that night in Nashville." He raised his hand to point ahead at a smudge of smoke which rolled into the air. "That's Hammerlock."

"What sort of town is it?"

"Wild, woolly and full of fleas, never been curried below the knees, or so it allows to be," drawled the scout. "I've known trail-end cattle and mining towns that could show it pointers for orneriness. Fact being there's livelier and there's more peaceable. It's not the sort of town your folks want to have much truck with. First thing I do when I get in is take a bath, get some new duds and go to see if Ole—"

The words ended abruptly, cut off by a soggy thud. Tom Blade jerked back in his saddle, hit the cantle, then slid to one side. The hole in the center of his chest was small but his back a bloody horror where the heavy caliber bullet smashed its way out. From the distance came the boom of a heavy rifle but Tom Blade did not hear it. He hit the ground in a limp pile and never moved again. Tom Blade had reached the place and put down his roots. His lifeblood stained and soaked the soil of the Arizona plain.

Colonel Raines came down from his saddle on the side away from the killer. Being neither a coward nor a fool he kept the horse between himself and the rocky outcrop from which the shot came. Quickly he drew the Henry rifle from his saddleboot but it would be of no use. The killer lay at least four hundred yards away, beyond any range the comparatively weak twenty-eight-grain load would carry. At any moment Raines expected to feel lead smash into him as the killer ended the job begun with Blade's death. Seconds ticked by and Raines thought he saw a movement on the rock but could not be sure. He became sure when a small dust cloud rolled into the air at the other side of the rock, enough to be caused by a fast-running horse. From the direction of the moving dust cloud, the killer appeared to be heading for Hammerlock.

Raines swung into his saddle again. One glance told him nothing but burying need to be done for Tom Blade. The killer would be beyond any range where he could be overtaken, so Raines decided his best bet would be to head for Hammerlock and allow the local law to handle the matter.

It was at that moment Raines became aware of the sound of rapidly approaching hooves coming from the direction of the train. A frown came to his face for he did not wish to have anyone asking questions. With that thought in mind, Raines turned his horse and rode to meet his daughter, wishing to prevent her going too close and seeing the bloody horror which was the late scout of the train.

Louise Raines rode with the easy grace of one long used to being in the saddle. She sat astride her bluegrass country thoroughbred instead of riding sidesaddle in the manner of a deep south young lady. Although not a tall girl, Louise showed signs of her father's proud and aristocratic features; yet she was beautiful and her face was fast becoming permanently tanned by the sun of the western plains. Her long blond hair was taken back in a bang, and a Stetson hat sat on her head. The white blouse and doeskin, divided skirt could not conceal the ripening curves of a young woman coming to maturity.

"What is it, papa?" Louise asked, halting at her father's side.

"Tom Blade was just shot," Raines replied, catching her arm. "No, Louise. He can't be helped. Ride back to the train and tell them to make camp by that stream back a piece. Tell Jim Lourde what happened and ask him to bring a burial detail. Go on, girl. Move!"

Turning her horse, Louise obeyed. During the trip west she had seen death through illness or accident, but not as a result of violence. That shape on the ground had been a man she knew, liked and respected. Louise felt numb and grief filled as she rode back toward the wagons.

After his daughter departed, Raines drew the Henry rifle from its boot and rode by Blade's body. Believing that the shot which killed the scout had been aimed at him, Raines wanted to get in close enough to use his Henry should the killer intend to make another try. No shot came; the killer had fled. So Raines did not ride up to the rock. Instead he swung clear of it so as to avoid spoiling any tracks which might lead to learning the killer's identity. Taking a roundabout route, Raines rode toward Hammerlock with the intention of reporting the shooting to the law. His route brought him into town on the opposite side to the train.

Hammerlock was a large town, by Arizona standards, boasting two main streets. Joined by numerous side alleys, the streets ran parallel and offered the usual selection of business premises. Coming in along Bisbee Street, Raines failed to see the sheriff's office and so turned his horse toward the Bell Saloon and halted with the intention of asking for directions.

A medium-sized, ugly man stood just inside the saloon.

After studying Raines for a moment, the man spoke over his shoulder, hitched up his gunbelt, which supported a brace of Starr Army revolvers, and pushed open the doors. Followed by half-a-dozen mean-looking cusses in cowhand clothing—although none probably ever handled rope or branding iron—the man left the saloon. A small crowd of passersby halted to watch the fun as the men fanned out in a half-circle around Raines and blocked his path.

"You bossing that she-bang out there?"

Raines turned at the words and looked the speaker over, then glanced at the other five who fanned out behind him.

"If you mean the wagon train, I am."

The hardcase grinned, thumb-hooking his hands into his gunbelt. "They tell me you gone shy a scout real sudden like," he said. "So I hereby offers me services."

Raines looked hard at the man. Nobody in Hammerlock could know about the killing of Tom Blade—except the man who killed him.

"How did you know Tom Blade was dead?" Raines asked.

Two men had come from the saloon and halted at the edge of the sidewalk to watch the fun. They made a contrasting yet in some ways much-alike pair. One was a handsome blond giant, three or more inches over six feet and with a great spread to his shoulders. He wore a costly white Stetson with a silver concha-decorated band around it. His hair was curly, golden blond in color and neatly trimmed. The face was handsome in the manner of a classic Greek god of old. Around his neck was a silk bandanna, tight rolled and hanging long ends over the made-to-measure tan shirt. His Levi's were also expensive and made to measure, as were his high-heeled, fancy-stitched boots. Around his waist was a brown leather gunbelt which hung just right, with holsters that told a tale, carrying a matched brace of ivory-handled 1860 Army Colts. That was the gunbelt and the way of wearing the same of a man real fast with a gun.

Beside such a fine figure, the second man hardly rated a second glance. Five-foot-six at most, although with width to his shoulders that hinted at strength, with dusty blond hair and a strong, handsome face. While expensive, he contrived to make his clothes look like nothing. Around his waist hung a good quality gunbelt with bone-handled Army Colts, butt forward in the holsters. Small he might be, yet he had the undefinable something which spelled tophand—if one troubled to look for it.

The two men, Texans, or their dress lied badly, stood side by side on the porch but made no move to interfere. They tensed slightly and exchanged glances on hearing Raines' question, then gave their full attention to the group in the street. In that brief exchange of glances, it seemed the tall man looked to the smaller for guidance in their next move.

The hardcase grinned over his shoulders at his backers. "He don't know who I am, boys. I'm Cultus Collins, Johnny Reb, that's who I am. I'm the worst pizen rattler this side of the Big Muddy, faster'n fast and twice as dangerous. I'm wuss th'n any grizzly b'ar, I am, and I'm your new scout."

"I never heard of you and I wouldn't take you to clean my scout's boots," Raines replied, forgetting for a moment he no longer had a scout.

"Be that right?" scoffed Collins. "Now is that right, boys. I puts it to you, be that nice?" He paused and went on when no answer came. "Here's me offering me invaluable services and he gets all uppy."

"Maybe needs teaching a lesson, Cultus," put in one of the five. "Make him do a dance for us."

Raines moved clear of his horse, the better to face the hardcase bunch. His hand lifted to knock open the flap of his holster but he knew his chances stood lower than nil. The Colonel was a good shot, capable of hitting his mark, but he needed his gun in his hand to do so. Often on the way west Tom Blade demonstrated how to draw and shoot in the frontier manner. Blade always claimed he should not set up to teach anybody such a vital piece of Western business for he surely was not fast with a gun, although Raines put the words down to modesty. One thing Raines did know for sure, fast or slow, Tom Blade's draw from an opened-top Western holster was better than anything Raines could do with his high riding, closed-top cavalry rig.

Collins' right hand moved and the Starr revolver was in it, his forefinger curling around the trigger, for the Starr was double-action and did not need the hammer thumb cocking.

The small Texan's left hand made a sight defying flip, crossing his body to bring the white-handled Army Colt from the right holster. The move was fast, very fast, the seven-and-half-inch-barreled Colt bellowing while only waist high, but the .44 bullet smashed the Starr from Collins' hand, sending it to the ground in the center of the street. Collins yelped and clutched at his hand, nursing it, for the lead from the Texan's bullet sprayed out on impact and peppered his skin.

Turning, Collins and his men faced the two Texans who stepped from the sidewalk and halted before them. The stocky hardcase's face was lined with a mixture of rage, pain and surprise that two men would risk stacking against him and his men.

"Who the hell asked you to put your bill in?" he snarled.

"We're in and in we stay," replied the small Texan, his voice an easy drawl. "Likewise asking about Tom Blade."

The Colt whirled on the trigger finger and went back into leather even as the words were spoken. Collins saw the move, saw his chance and ran his tongue tip over his lips. His left hand came from the injured right to hover over the butt of his second Starr. Behind him the men tensed, ready to take cards in the game. Six to two were good odds and the man who stood at the end of the saloon building was an ace in the hole. Collins gave fast thought to the matter. He was fair with a gun but knew he was faced by two who were even better. Only having Hooks Hammer standing to one side and behind the two Texans would give him nerve enough to stack against them.

It was at that moment, in a fast-taken glance, Collins discovered his ace in the hole was no longer a sure-winning card.

The tough on the sidewalk saw the interference to Collins' plans and knew it was time to take cards in the game. His hand dropped to the butt of his gun, the fingers curling around it. Then his hat was thrust from his head from behind. Fingers dug into his long, bay rum-smelling hair and hauled his head back to hit against the post he leaned on. Something which glinted in the sun passed before his eyes, disappeared from his sight to go under his beard and rest against his throat.

Then the small man stood still, very still. That glinting thing which now rested with a feather-light touch on his throat had only been in view for a brief instant but he knew full well what it was. He knew the eleven and a half inch length, two and a half inch width of the blade of a genuine James Black bowie knife when he saw one. He knew also that such a knife, forged by the Arkansas master, held an edge many a barber's razor might envy. He also knew the thing which passed before his eyes and was now in a position for the speedy slitting of his throat was a James Black bowie knife. Nor did he nurse any foolish dreams that it was the rounded upper edge of the blade which touched him. It was the blade, the cutting edge and he stood very still because of this.

"Go ahead, *hombre!*" a gentle voice purred in his ear, sounding meaner than the snarl of a she-cougar defending her young. "Just try and pull it."

Collins saw his hole card taken out of the game and felt suddenly uneasy at the appearance of the man who took Hammer out. Man might not be the right word for the knife-holding Texan for he looked very young. He was a tall, slim, wiry youngster yet gave the impression of having whipcord strength. His clothing was all black, from his head to high-heeled boots. Even his gunbelt was black, as was the sheath from which the knife came and the holster in which hung, butt forward, an old walnut-handled Second

Model Colt Dragoon revolver. His hair was as black as the wing of a deep south crow. His face Indian dark, almost babyishly handsome and young looking except for his eyes. They were cold eyes, red-hazel in color. They were eyes which looked far too old for so young a face. That dark, somehow Indian-looking boy might look about sixteen years, but if that was his true age they were sixteen hard-packed and dangerous years.

So with his hole card gone, Collins was left with the choice of backing water and getting clear fast or sitting tight and trying to force the game to go the way he planned it. All he and his men needed to do was stack against the two Texans, for Raines did not come into his calculations at all. Long before he could draw the gun from its holster he would be dead. That meant only two men stood between Collins and his plan. The third man being fully occupied with holding Hooks Hammer could not cut in. It was for Collins to make the play; the others would back him in it.

Then a man in the crowd spoke, the words sounding clear in the chilling silence as the crowd prepared to head for cover fast.

"That's him," said the man, excitement in his tones. "That small Texan. I saw him when he was the law in Quiet Town. That's him. It's Dusty Fog."

CHAPTER TWO

Louise Finds Trouble

RIDING back to the wagon, Louise Raines met and informed her father's second-in-command, Jim Lourde, and Doctor Fremont of Blade's death. The men agreed to fetch the body back for burial and Lourde signaled to the leading wagon to start turning for the night's circle. Face dull and showing the grief she felt, Louise watched her father's colored servant in the lead wagon swinging his team off the line of march.

"Hey Louise!"

The girl turned and saw a woman waving to her from one of the wagons as it went by. She rode alongside Maisie Simons' wagon, for the older woman was her best friend. Maisie was something of a mystery to the other travelers, for she was not one of the original party but joined them in Nashville. She was a small, shapely and not bad looking woman in her early thirties. Her hair was mousy brown and her tanned face usually wore a smile. She dressed in the same style as the other women but was much more worldly than most of them. For all that Maisie led a blameless life on the train. She kept her wagon in good condition and the three Chinese helpers were no trouble. Her reason for going west was to start a small café. Why she decided to go, or why to travel with this train was something she never mentioned and nobody asked her.

From the start Maisie and Louise had got on together, although the girl was aware her father did not entirely approve of the friendship. Maisie knew much of living in a wagon and helped the girl. Right now Louise wanted someone to talk with and discuss what happened to Tom Blade.

With surprising agility Maisie dropped from her slowly moving wagon. The Chinese driver gave no sign of ever knowing she was gone but carried on following the preceding wagon around in the circle.

"What's wrong, Louise?"

Louise did not know her face showed so much. She told Maisie of the killing of Tom Blade and the woman's mouth lost its smile. There was little change in her expression, however, and her voice was gentle as she asked:

"Where's your father now?"

"He waited for the men to—"

Louise began to reply, then stopped, for she saw three riders coming, one leading a horse over which hung a tarp-wrapped figure. Louise gave a gasp for her father was not with them. She whirled the horse and rode away before Maisie could say another word. The woman watched her go for a moment, then turned and went after her own wagon.

"Where's papa?" Louise asked the men, trying not to look at the thing over the saddle.

"Must have gone to the town for the law, Miss Louise," Lourde replied.

He almost immediately wished he had said nothing for the girl sent her horse by them and was riding fast across the range.

"Where're you going, Louise?" shouted the doctor.

"To town after papa. You know how quick tempered he is."

The men knew all right. They also knew Louise was like

her father in that when she made up her mind, she let nothing stand in her way.

"One of us should go after her," Lourde growled. "But I don't want to take men from the train. You know what it's like around these towns."

Fremont nodded. It was always wise to have a strong guard when this near to a town. More so in the case of a rough town like Hammerlock was reported to be. In such a town would be men who regarded a wagon train like this as a god-sent opportunity to collect loot, horses or livestock.

"Leave it for a spell," the third man suggested. "Miss Louise's a sensible enough girl. She won't run into any trouble and will likely find her father with the sheriff. She'll be able to keep the Colonel calm if he gets hot headed."

"All right. If she's not back by dark I'll send some of the men to look for her," Lourde growled. "Now let's get down to doing what needs to be done."

Holding her horse to a fast trot, Louise headed toward where rising smoke marked the site of Hammerlock. She did not know that her father took a roundabout route and felt worried at not seeing him. Knowing his quick temper, she wanted to be at his side and exert a soothing influence should chance bring him face to face with Blade's killer.

With growing concern, Louise rode into town along Prescott Street and still saw no sign of her father. She looked for the sheriff's office, not knowing that it lay on a side street; the citizens not wishing to have open, flaunting law and order in the business sections, as this might damage their image as a wide-open town where anything went, such being good for trade.

A crowd of men burst from a saloon, a bunch of wildly excited spectators to a pair of fighting cowhands. They erupted into the street before Louise, milling about and spilling into the street.

The girl brought her horse to a halt. It was a spirited and highly strung animal, not used to having excited crowds leaping about, yelling and waving their hands or hats before its face. So the horse started to fiddlefoot and rear. Louise slipped from the saddle, holding the reins and trying to calm the horse. She showed that she was not in a panic for she took time to toss the reins over the hitching rail and tied them, leaving both hands to soothe the horse while preventing it from bolting.

One of the fighters swung a wild punch which sent the other sprawling back through the batwing doors of the saloon. With a wild yell the cowhand plunged after his opponent and the crowd started to surge after them not wishing to miss the fun. Almost all of the crowd that is.

"Now ain't this a purty sight, Sam?" asked a voice.

"Purty as a June bug, Homer," came the reply in a drink-slurred voice. "Yes, sir, as purty as a June bug."

Louise turned to look at the speakers. They stood on the edge of the sidewalk and the girl knew both carried a full load of coffin varnish. They were a pair of bull-whackers from their dress and appearance. One was tall and hefty, the other shorter though even broader and while fat, did not look soft or flabby. On their faces, unhidden by a week of whisker-growings, was the truculent look of men who were drunk enough to be primed for any kind of trouble.

The taller of the two men swung from the sidewalk and stepped toward the girl. The other man grinned, then also stepped down to move forward.

"Yes, sir, Sam," said the tall man. "This here's a real fine looking gal."

"Wonder if she kisses as well as she looks?" asked Sam. "What you reckon, Homer. Reckon she would?"

"Ain't but the one way to find out," Homer replied, moving toward Louise with his hands held ready to grip her.

Louise gave a gasp of fright as she backed away. Then her shoulders hit the hitching rail and she could go no further. The man was coming toward her; she could smell the stale sweat and bad whisky and his whiskery face loomed above her. Louise was scared, more scared than she'd ever been in her life.

There were few onlookers on the sidewalk and none of

them offered to help the girl. The men on the sidewalk were town dwellers and they were not aiming to tangle with a pair of bad mean drunks to help a strange girl. She would get kissed but nothing more would come of the matter, not in the streets in plain daylight. No Hammerlock citizen was going to antagonize men who were good customers in town, especially if doing so was likely to get them hurt.

Luckily for Louise that sentiment only applied to townsmen. The man who swung from the sidewalk and moved forward was no town dweller. He was a cowhand and a Texas man or his clothing lied. It showed from his low-crowned, wide-brimmed J. B. Stetson hat, in the multihued bandanna around his throat, in his short Levi's, star-decorated boots. It showed also in the buscadero gunbelt around his waist and the butt forward, walnut-handled Army Colts in his holsters. He was a red-haired young man with a freckled, pugnaciously handsome face, the sort of face which only looks right with a broad grin on it. The grin was still in evidence as he moved forward, although it was a tight lipped and hard grin.

"All right," he said and if there was any doubt as to his place of origin it was dispelled the moment he opened his mouth. His drawl was Texas, pleasant and yet grim in undertone. "Let loose!""

The two toughs looked at the rash intruder, one look being all they needed to know this was the real thing and not some dressed-up kid trying to act like a knight in shining armor and rescuing the maiden in distress. There was a heft to the tall young Texan's build which told of hard muscle under his hide. There was a look about the way his guns hung which warned the bull-whackers he was their match and more in any matter of "triggernometry." They were fist-fighters, only wearing their guns for defending themselves against Indian attack, not for fighting in town.

"Now who asked you to horn in?" asked Sam, sticking his face forward in an open invitation for the Texan to do something about it.

He did. His hand came up against Sam's face and shoved

hard. Taken by surprise, Sam staggered backward and sat down hard on the sidewalk. His drunken mind could not accept that any man dare tangle with him, so the Texan's direct and forceful action threw him right off balance. To the drunken Sam it was as if a sheep turned and attacked a mountain lion without provocation and his brain could neither understand the situation nor give the necessary directions to his limbs in the matter of dealing with the Texan.

"Get away from that girl!" barked the Texan.

Louise clenched her fists, preparing to sell her honor dearly, for the big man's hands rested on either side of her shoulders, pinning her to the hitching rail while his face came nearer. She heard the Texan's words, saw the sudden anger on Homer's face as he also heard and the meaning sank through to his brain. His hands came from the rail and he turned.

Homer looked at the tall Texan, his eyes glowed with sudden rage, aided by the load of Old Scalp Lifter he carried. Unable to deal with more than one thing at a time, Homer's eyes took in the Texan and did not see Sam sitting in a dazed manner on the sidewalk. So Homer wondered why the Texan stood there instead of being stomped into the street by Sam's bootheels. One thing Homer knew for sure, that red-haired Texan was shoving his face into something that did not concern him. Homer decided to remove the face forcibly and alter its shape considerably.

With that thought in mind he growled, "Yeah!"

Saying it, he swung his fist, only that proved to be the wrong thing to do. The fist, thrown by a powerful arm and body, was slow, although the result would have been highly satisfactory had the blow landed. The redhead's left hand came up and deflected the punch sending it harmlessly over his shoulder. Then his right hand lashed out, shooting forward with the full weight of his body behind it and a clear brain to guide it. His clenched fist exploded on Homer's bristle-covered jaw, snapping the man's head back with a click like two king-sized billiard balls coming together. The difference in style showed in that blow, for where Homer used only muscle, the Texan hit with speed, precision, aim and muscle. It would have written a finish to Homer's fighting capabilities for some time had the Texan been able to follow it up. As it was the blow put Homer out of action for a few moments which suddenly became vital to the Texan's well-being.

Even while the Texan moved in to finish Homer off in the approved manner, Sam took a hand. His partner hung on the hitching rail, eyes glassy and head shaking in an attempt to regain control on a world which appeared to roar around in circles. Sam saw this as he lunged forward with his arms held wide. The Texan did not see the fresh danger and heard Louise's warning cry an instant too late. His intention to move in and make sure Homer did not come back into the fight was forgotten as he found himself with trouble on his hands.

Sam came in with a speed out of keeping in one of his bulk and possible liquid content. The bull-whacker's arms were locked around the Texan's waist before he could defend himself and in a crushing bear hug which had brought Sam victorious through more than one fight.

Louise gasped in horror. She saw the Texan's face twist in agony as the arms crushed down on him. His hands thrust under Sam's chin forcing the head back but not breaking the grip around him. Grunting again, Sam squeezed harder; he heard the Texan's gasp of pain and grinned savagely. Then the Texan changed his grip, his hands going under Sam's chin and his thumbs gouging into the fat flesh of the throat, cutting Sam's breath abruptly with the steel-hard fingers. Sam's next crush lacked the power of the others. In his present condition, due to the whisky, having his breath cut off in such a manner ended his attack. The Texan tore free and thrust Sam backward. In a continuance of the thrust, the Texan's right hand smashed into Sam's stomach bringing a grunt of pain and folding him over. The right fist drove up in a whistling blow which lifted Sam erect and over, back to the sidewalk edge where he sat down hard once more.

Homer moved from the hitching rail, still dazed as he dropped his hand to the butt of his revolver, trying to haul it free of leather. The Texan pivoted around, his right hand turning palm out to bring the walnut-handled Colt from his right side, throwing down on Homer in a fast-done cavalry twist hand draw.

"You can have it that way too," he warned.

Homer's drunken condition prevented his seeing the danger. He still tried to get out his gun even though he would be too late. Louise closed her eyes, for she expected to hear the roar of a shot and had no wish to see a man killed. She thought her rescuer would not hesitate to use his Colt. He used it, but not in the way she expected. Instead of shooting he stepped forward and swung the gun around. The Texan struck hard but not with the barrel, for the 1860 Army Colt's ramrod lever, lying under the barrel, might be damaged by striking something like a human head. Instead he brought his arm around and crashed his fist like a hammer's head, the butt of the Colt crashing into Homer's jaw. The big drunk spun around in a full circle, smashed into the rail again by Louise's side with his eyes glazed over. His legs buckled under him and he slid down to the ground. From the way he went down, it did not appear likely he would rise for some time.

Sam came up again and attacked. Anger brought him forward in a wild rush with his fists swinging. The Texan avoided the wild-swung blows, his right hand, still holding the Colt, swung under the man's arms and thudded home into his belly with the boom of a bass drum when struck by the stick. Sam had hard belly muscles protected by rolls of fat but they'd been soaked in a whisky-jag and he could not take a blow of that kind. Sober he might have fought on after such a blow, but not in his present state. Croaking in agony Sam sank to his knees, holding his injured stomach and gasping for breath.

The Colt pinwheeled on the Texan's finger, twisted and went back into the holster. He moved toward Sam who, still holding his stomach with one hand, tried to force himself to his feet. The Texan took careful aim and threw his left fist with the power of a mule-kick against the side of the bull-whacker's jaw. Sam's body hurled to one side, crashing to the ground and looking as if he tried to plough up the street with his ear. He lit down spread out flat and did not offer to rise; in fact he did not move at all.

Working his fingers to get the use back into them the Texan turned toward Louise. He was breathing hard and once his hands would work again he touched his ribs. A wry grin came to his face and Louise moved forward. Her legs felt weak and shaky and her hand trembled but she gained control of herself.

"Are you all right?" she asked.

"I've felt better, ma'am," he replied and the grin grew even broader. "Like one time when a hoss throwed me, then walked back over me. Sure, reckon I felt some better then."

"Are you badly hurt?"

"I'll likely live. The boys though, they didn't mean no hurt. Just been taking on too much bottled trouble and bravemaker. Can I help you?"

Louise felt a momentary panic. If the redhead acted as had the other two she would be in a far worse position for nobody would dare help her after seeing how he handled the two men. Then sense came back to the girl. The young man spoke with a southern drawl and showed no signs of being drunk. His offer of help came in the best possible spirit. She heard a shot somewhere beyond the noisy saloon and her hands clenched nervously.

"Easy ma'am," drawled the Texan. "There'll be no more trouble from them two for a spell. You'll be long gone before they wake up."

"Thank you," she gasped. "But that shot—"

"Shucks, in a town like this there's always likely to be somebody fooling and shooting off guns."

The easy relaxed tones did something to steady Louise's nerves down. She looked at the grinning freckled face and liked what she saw in it. He was a pleasant enough sounding

young man and she decided to trust him, to ask for his help.
If she was to find her father she would need help, for she'd
already seen the sort of trouble a girl could get herself into
in such a town.

"Have you seen a rather tall man wearing a Confederate
officer's campaign hat, buckskin jacket, riding pants and
boots come along this way?" she asked, then remembered
a vital piece of information. "He was riding a big bay
thoroughbred stallion."

In a western town a fine horse would attract more attention than its rider.

"No ma'am, can't say I have," replied the Texan, although he gave the girl a searching glance. "Which same
I've been wedded to that hitching rail pretty constant for
a couple of hours and he hasn't come by in that time."

The girl felt suddenly afraid, sure her father lay dead
somewhere on the open range. She knew she must get help
to find him and the Texan was the only man she might trust
in the town.

"Could you help me find him, please?" she gasped.

"I'd surely admire to, ma'am. There's another street back
of here. Reckon we might try looking on it."

The girl felt relieved for she did not know of Bisbee
Street. She unfastened her horse's reins and led it as she
walked with the Texan around the side of the saloon and
through the gap between the buildings.

They came on to Bisbee Street and looked along it. One
way was clear but down the other they saw a group of men
standing in the center of the street. Louise gave a gasp as
she saw her father in the group. There were three Texas
cowhands in a group around her father and even as she
looked Louise saw the group of men facing her father turn
and walk into a saloon.

"Who are those three men?" Louise asked, sure they
were picking on her father and the others had been prevented
from helping him. It was a foolish question, she thought
as soon as she spoke; the redhead could hardly be expected
to know everyone in town.

Apparently he did know, for he replied. "The three worst varmints this side of the Big Muddy. If that's your pappy he's in tolerable bad company."

Louise waited to hear no more but headed across the street to save her father.

CHAPTER THREE

Tom Blade's Friends

DUSTY FOG. Just two words, but they stiffened Cultus Collins' hand, froze it over the butt of his gun. Behind him his men stood stiff, still, making sure no movement of their hands would give the Texan cause to be suspicious. They could hardly believe this was Dusty Fog, although all of them knew the name and what it stood for in the West.

Dusty Fog. There was a name to conjure with in the West. First as a cavalry captain at seventeen leading his gray-clad troop against the Union Army in the War. In that, his name ranked with John Singleton Mosby or Turner Ashby as a cavalry leader and a master of light cavalry tactics. Then after the War Dusty Fog's name became known as a cowhand tophand, a master of the cowboy trade. He was segundo of the great OD Connected ranch in the Rio Hondo country of Texas, leader of the elite of the crew, Ole Devil Hardin's floating outfit, two members of which were with him now. He was known as a trail boss, learned his trade under the master of the cattle-trailing art, Colonel Charlie Goodnight, and now was said to be the equal of his teacher at the business. He'd been town marshal of Quiet Town and backed by his loyal friends brought law and order to that wild, wide open town where three lesser men tried and paid for their failure with their lives. That then was Dusty Fog. Yet there was even more to his capabilities. It was rumored that he knew certain alien yet effective fighting arts which rendered bigger and stronger men helpless before his bare hands. It was more than rumored that he was lightning fast with his matched Colts and capable of hitting his mark at the end of the half second it took him to draw and shoot.

This was the man who cut in on the game of Cultus Collins. A small man who towered over the heads of the tallest in the crowd.

By a simple process of thought, the name of that blond giant and the black-dressed boy also became clear. The big blond was Mark Counter, for where Dusty Fog stood Mark Counter was most likely to be. The knowledge gave no comfort to Collins and his men for Mark Counter had made a name in his own right.

He was said to be one of the finest fist-fighters in the West and able to meet any man on any terms. His strength brought him the reputation of being a rangeland Hercules. He was known as a tophand, if anything, better with cattle than was his pard, Dusty Fog. He was good with a rifle and men who knew said he was very good with his matched, ivory-butted Colts. One thing was for sure, men who knew said he was almost as fast as Dusty Fog.

The third man, still holding his bowie knife to the throat of Hooks Hammer, was just as well known. The Ysabel Kid, that was a name still spoken with awe down on the Rio Grande border. He was a wild young heller and quite likely to use the knife if the other man gave him the slightest cause to do so. The Kid's father had been a wild Irish-Kentuckian and his mother was the daughter of Long Walker, the Comanche chief and his French-Creole squaw. It was from such a mixture of bloods that the Ysabel Kid was born. From his father he inherited a rugged, indepen-

dent nature and the sighting eye of an eagle. His skilled use
of the Winchester Model of 1866 rifle was a legend as was
his knowledge of the art of cut and slash in the manner of
the old master James Bowie himself. He was fair with his
old Dragoon Colt in a land where to be fair meant to be
able to draw, shoot and make a hit in a second. However,
he preferred the other two weapons for offense and defense
and only called on the four-pound, thumb-busting Dragoon
when the others would not serve his needs. He was less of
a cowhand than the other two, his particular field having
to do with riding scout. In this he was aided by his Indian
blood, a knowledge of six tribal tongues, mastery of fluent
Spanish and the ability to read sign where a buck Apache
would not know how to begin. All in all Loncey Dalton
Ysabel was a good man to have as a friend, for he made
a real bad enemy.

The Kid released his hold of the man and Hammer staggered forward. Then with a gesture of supreme contempt
the Kid sheathed his knife, walked along the sidewalk and
joined his two friends.

"How did you know about Tom Blade being shot?"
Raines asked.

Collins licked his lips again in a nervous manner. His
eyes went first to Raines, then to the three Texans.

"I heard somebody talking," he answered lamely.

"Who?" asked Dusty Fog.

"Some man who came into town in a hurry and rode on
through," Collins replied without any great conviction.

"You wouldn't be lying, now would you, *pelado*?" asked
the Kid in a mild voice which held neither mildness nor
kindness to Collins' listening ears.

"That's how we heard."

Collins ignored the insult the Kid laid on him although
he spoke enough Mexican to know what *pelado* meant. It
was used to mean a thief of the lowest kind, one who would
rob the bodies of the dead. Collins knew this, knew the
insult but there was not enough pride in the world to make
him call the Kid down to avenge it.

"Where'd this *hombre* go, happen he ever came?" asked Mark Counter, his voice deep and cultured as became the son of the owner of one of the biggest spreads in the Texas Big Bend country. Mark could have been on his father's ranch but was content to stay at the OD Connected and work with his friends.

"Headed on out of town right after he told it," Collins replied.

Dusty Fog watched the faces of the men backing Collins. They did not know for sure what was going on. Collins was the only one who knew anything about this business on hand; the others were just with him.

"Why'd you jump this gent?" asked Dusty.

"Shucks, we thought he might need another scout and I want work," Collins answered. "Only I didn't like his way of answering a man so I was all set to have some sport with him."

"Did yuh? Now how'd you like to take the same sport with me?"

Collins shook his head violently. "I ain't fussing none with you, Cap'n Fog. I was only funning."

"Well I'm not," Dusty drawled, his voice gentle as the first whisper of a Texas blue northern storm and heralding the start of something just as dangerous. "Drift, *hombre*. We're riding out to where Tom was killed and Lon'll cut for sign. If we find anything that points to who killed Tom we'll be back."

"Which same you can surely stake your money on," agreed Mark Counter.

Collins and his men withdrew, heading back into the saloon they'd just vacated. Collins left his busted Starr gun where it lay on the ground, for he did not wish to stand on the order of his going. The Kid's victim joined the other men and faded into the bar, allowing the batwing doors to swing to behind him.

Dusty turned to face Raines after the men went from sight. "I'm Dusty Fog, this's Mark Counter and the Ysabel Kid."

"I thought I recognized you, Captain Fog," Raines replied, holding out his hand. "I saw you in the War. I heard about you, too." The Colonel's eyes went to Mark, "You're the one who brought that damned skirtless tunic into the army. I called you a few names over that."

"You weren't the only one, sir," replied Mark with a grin.

In the War Mark's taste in uniforms did not entirely agree with dress regulations but found favor among the young bloods of the South. Then, as now, Mark was something of a Beau Brummel and his style of dress was much copied by his fellows.

The grin died for there was something more important on hand.

"About Tom Blade, sir?"

Raines opened his mouth to reply, wondering how they knew his rank. Then there was somebody standing between him and the three Texas men. A slim blond girl, with flashing eyes, fists clenched and the attitude of a she-bobcat defending her young, faced Dusty, Mark and the Kid.

"You wretched bullies!" Louise Raines blazed at Mark as being the most likely leader of the proposed attack on her father. She directed the speech at all three but Mark most of all. "How dare you bully and browbeat my father, you great hulking brutal savage."

Mark was taken back by the girl's fury. He was not used to presentable and pretty young women taking such an attitude with him when he first met them. His two friends looked on with grins of amusement and admiration.

"You tell him, ma'am," drawled the Kid, not knowing what was wrong but willing to enjoy it to the full.

The words were ill timed for they brought the fury of Louise's attack on the Kid's head.

"Be quiet!" she hissed. "You're as bad as he is. I suppose you think it a great joke to pick on a man old enough to be—"

Raines was surprised to see his daughter in the town and more than surprised at the spirited way in which she leaped to his defense. However, he knew he must stop her for she was heaping abuse on three innocent heads. He caught the girl by the arm and turned her to face him. The three Texans were grinning broadly, for they knew a mistake had been made, although they were not sure how.

"Louise!" Raines barked. "Stop it this instant. These young men helped me out of a difficult position. They're friends."

"I know they are," she replied, so angry that the words did not sink in. "I'll not have—I—" the words ended and the girl's face turned even more red as she realized what she'd said and done. "Gracious to Betsy, what have I been doing, papa?"

The Ysabel Kid laughed, looking about fourteen years old. "You done good, ma'am. Real good."

"I've never seen it done better," Mark agreed, sweeping off his hat.

"Shucks ma'am," Dusty went on. "I sure can't help having such villainous-looking friends."

Raines scowled at his daughter. "You owe these gentlemen an apology, girl."

"No, sir," objected Mark. "The lady was only doing what she thought was the right thing."

It was then Louise remembered her rescuer and started to turn, saying, "But you told me—"

The words ended unfinished for the red-haired cowhand had disappeared and she could see no sign of him anywhere.

"Who told you what, ma'am?" asked Dusty. "Say, let's get off the street and let the traffic through, shall we?"

They all stepped on to the sidewalk and the crowd dispersed about their own business for all could see there would be nothing more happening. Louise told quickly of her fright and rescue, describing the redhead in flattering terms. The description brought knowing nods from Mark and the Kid.

"I thought so, Mark," drawled the Kid, sounding deadly serious. "It was him."

"Sure sounds that way," agreed Mark just as seriously.

Louise looked from one man to the other and gasped, "Who?"

"Red Blaze," explained Mark.

"As ever was," said the Kid. "A wilder, woollier varmint never drew breath of good Texas air."

"Is he an outlaw?" gasped Louise.

"Worse'n that, ma'am," the Kid drawled, his voice suggesting Red Blaze's social standing came well below that of the worst kind of outlaw. "I don't reckon outlaw even starts to cover it one lil bit at all."

The girl gulped. She did not see Dusty's smile and the twinkle which came into her father's eyes for her full attention was upon the other two.

"Well," she snapped, just a hint of defiance in her tones. "He looked and acted like a perfect gentleman."

"Don't let that worry you," warned Mark. "It's his favorite trick."

"Do you think that man Collins knows anything about Tom's death, Captain Fog?" asked Raines.

"Likely, sir. But if we'd tried to force the issue there'd have been lead thrown and I don't want that. Take it kindly if you'd show us where Tom died."

"Of course I will. Where's your horse, Louise?"

The girl suddenly realized she no longer led her horse. Turning she saw it standing across the street with its reins hanging before it and Mark collected it for her. On returning Mark joined the others as they headed for one of the livery barns to collect their horses. Colonel Raines remembered he had not introduced his daughter to the Texans and performed the introduction as they walked along.

Louise stared at Dusty as if she could hardly believe her eyes and ears. In the War Dusty's name ranked high and she'd often heard tell of his exploits. He had been one of her heroes, a knight in the dress uniform of the Confederate Army instead of shining armor and carrying a Haiman Brothers saber in place of a lance. She always thought of him as a tall, magnificently handsome man on a huge black stallion, leading his loyal troop against the hated Yankees.

It came as something of a shock to discover this small and insignificant man was Captain Dustine Edward Marsden Fog of Troop "C," Texas Light Cavalry.

Louise knew her father wished to talk with Dusty; so did the other two and they both drew back pouring stories of the notorious Red Blaze into her receptive ears. Dusty and Raines walked in front, discussing the situation at the train.

Louise felt relieved as they rode from town, Dusty astride a seventeen hand paint stallion which matched Mark's huge blood-bay stud horse in size and shape. The Kid rode afork a magnificent white stallion fully as large as the other two and looking meaner than a bull-elk bugling for mates in the middle of the rut. The Kid warned Louise never to lay a hand on his horse but she did not need the warning. All her life had been spent around horses and she knew a bad one when she saw it.

Each man's saddle was a low-horned, double-girthed range rig; no Texan used the word "cinch." To each horn was strapped a rope, and a bedroll hung from each cantle. Each owned one of the improved Henry rifles, the gun fast becoming known by its new name, Winchester. Dusty's weapon proved to be in the carbine size, while the other two carried rifles proper.

On collecting the horses from the livery barn, Louise had failed to notice a fourth Texas saddle on the burro by the wall. Likewise she paid no attention to the huge clay-bank stallion in the next stall to Dusty's paint. If she'd noticed the horse she might also have seen the brand it carried; an O and a D, the straight edge of the D touching the side of the O.

"We'll look around first," Dusty said as they reached the rock where the killer hid. "See what we can learn."

"And then?" asked Raines.

"That depends on what we find."

They all dismounted but only the Kid went forward on foot. His eyes studied the ground with care. Halting by one scrubby bush the Kid examined its branches, then under and all around it. He moved on, checked the rock in the same manner and with equal care, missing nothing the human eyes could see. Finally he dropped to the ground and gave a low whistle. The huge white stallion tossed its head and moved forward, answering the call which was almost too low for human ears to catch.

"What a horse," Louise breathed. "Would Lon sell him?"

"Not for all the money in the world," Dusty replied, giving a sign, and the others moved forward on foot.

The Kid had returned to the bush and waited for them. He waved a hand toward it and Louise tried to see what interested the dark youngster.

"Hoss was tied here for a spell. Light bay I'd guess. Feller got down and went to that rock there. Feller about five-foot-eight or nine I'd reckon. Be there for at least one hour, maybe longer. He stayed up there on the rock and didn't come down at all."

"How can you tell?" asked Louise.

"He left some sign behind," answered the Kid, pointing to faint marks on a branch. "Reins made those. Hoss droppings tells me how long he stayed, near enough, and when they left. The hoss brushed against the bush and left enough hair for me to know its color. Then this *hombre* walked across here," the Kid led the way pointing to the ground. At the rock his finger stabbed out to indicate some faint scratches. "Went up this way."

"Was it Collins?" Mark asked.

The Kid threw a withering look at his big pard and sarcasm dripped from his voice as he replied, "I know I'm about as smart as a Texan can get, which same's real smart. But I can't work miracles 'cepting on every third Sunday of the month. How in hell would I know if it was Collins or somebody we never heard tell of?"

"What do you reckon?" Dusty interrupted. "You're getting worse'n a Yankee congressman way you talk on and on."

The Kid extracted a cigarette Mark just finished rolling from the big Texan's fingers, ignoring a remark that it was long gone time he bought some of his own.

"It could have been Collins. It's about the right stride for him."

"How would you know that?" Louise asked.

"Length of stride. Whoever it was lay up there on that rock with his rifle rested like he didn't aim to miss what he aimed at. He shot Tom, slid down and lit out at a dead run."

Raines knew something of tracking but compared with the Kid he knew himself to be the veriest beginner. From what little he could read on the ground Raines knew the Kid was most likely calling the game right.

"Does Collins use a Sharps?" asked Mark Counter of nobody in particular, as he stood by the rock and looked down.

The Kid grinned. "I wondered if you'd see that."

"See what?" demanded Louise.

The Kid bent and pointed to the ground just at the side of the rock. In the earth which was softened by water running from the rock surface was a small depression which she could not identify. She raised a puzzled face toward the Kid who was straightened up by her side.

"He rested his rifle there. That's the mark the butt-plate made, him not standing it muzzle down. That mark's too big for a Henry or a Spencer and not the right shape for a Hawken or Mississippi rifle, happen one of them could carry the range the Colonel allows Tom was dropped at. Fact being the rifle has to be one that'll carry over four hundred yards. That means a metal cartridge, single-shot rifle like either a Sharps or a Remington."

"Which same means we'll have to see what sort of rifle Mr. Collins totes," Mark put in. "If he has one—"

"He'll be a danged sight more loco than I reckoned," growled the Kid, then joined the Colonel and Dusty. "Way she reads to me this *hombre* wanted Tom, not you, Colonel. Happen he'd wanted both he could have dropped you both. But he only stayed long enough to put lead into Tom, then lit out without even reloading."

"You can't know that for sure," Raines objected.

"A Sharps or a Remington throws out its empty shells and they land some place. Which same there's none around here. Way you told it he didn't stay long enough to find it after he shot."

Mark threw a disgusted look at the Kid then turned to Louise. "He sounds like a regular Pinkerton sneak, doesn't he. Can't you just see him sneaking up to an old widow-woman to learn all her secrets?"

Louise gave a gurgle of amusement at the thought. Her eyes went from one to another of the three Texans. They were such self-reliant men and she felt that she could trust them with her life. Dusty Fog no longer impressed her as being small, he never did again; never would she think of his size in mere inches. To her, as to all his friends, Dusty Fog stood the tallest of them all. Mark Counter would certainly set the hearts fluttering among the young unmarried women of the train when they saw him. So would the Kid, although she doubted if he was the sort of young man their mothers would approve of knowing. Her rescuer in town, despite all the things Mark and the Kid told about him, was the same kind of man, polite, friendly and courteous. He must have been driven to his life of crime by the Yankees in that hell period just after the War when reconstructionists ruled Texas. She hoped she might meet the man called Red Blaze once more and try to turn him from his bad ways.

"I'd like you to come back to the train with me," Raines suggested.

On his way to the rock Raines had told the three Texans nothing beyond the killing of the scout. Now he knew he was going to need help. He would get it better if he laid his cards on the table and allowed Dusty Fog to see the entire hand as it was dealt.

"That's what Uncle Devil sent us out here to do," Dusty replied. "Tom Blade wrote Uncle Devil from Nashville and asked for help. We were out on a chore but Uncle Devil telegraphed us to meet up with you. We picked on Hammerlock as being the most likely place to find you and came direct instead of searching the plains for you."

Raines frowned. "I didn't know Tom had been in touch with General Hardin."

"He was like that, Tom, kind of close mouthed. But he was a friend and I aim to get the killer."

"Would you help me get the train through to Backsight?"

"As soon as we find the man who downed Tom," promised Dusty. "We'll head back to Hammerlock with what we know and ask some questions. There's no more law in town than hair on a billiard ball so we'll handle things our own way."

"The man responsible for killing Tom is in Backsight," Raines pointed out.

"That takes some believing, sir," drawled Mark. "Lon's ole Nigger hoss here can run faster'n any I ever saw over a distance and even he couldn't make Backsight since Tom was shot."

The other two Texans gave their agreement but Raines shook his head. "The man who hired whoever did the killing is in Backsight. I was the one the shot was meant for and there were three earlier attempts on my life."

Louise gave a gasp for this was something not even she knew about. The three Texans showed no surprise. From all their faces showed that hearing people say attempts had been made on their lives was no novelty.

"I don't buy it being a try at you, Colonel," the Kid put in. "I might not be able to tell the difference between you and Tom at say two miles, but it'd show like a nigger on a snowbank close up. You ride like a cavalryman and Tom slouched western style in his saddle. That *hombre* was using a rest for his rifle which same means he aimed to hit what he shot at. The bullet was meant for Tom, not you."

"I've told you something about how I came to be bringing this train," Raines said. "I didn't tell you that I was warned about coming the same day I received a letter from the land agent in Backsight. It was a letter from a man called Terry Ortega, although it was unsigned."

"How'd you know who it was from if it wasn't signed?" asked the Kid.

"The letter was written in pencil and on the back of it

I found the marks left by having a second sheet on top of it. The top sheet had been used to write Terry Ortega's address and the pencil point marked through it on to the sheet I received. I ignored it until a knife was thrown at me and just missed my head. The next day I found a note in the same handwriting, it said they'd missed me that time but wouldn't miss again if I tried to take the train to Backsight. I thought of holding up the train until we could get the Arizona law to investigate but there wasn't time. So we moved out when arranged. There were two more tries at killing me, once in Louisville when a heavy wagon almost ran me down and later in Nashville when someone took a shot at me. Each time I received a warning note."

"Yet it was Tom who died," Dusty pointed out. "Do you know who this Ortega is or anything about him?"

"The land agent's sister is traveling with us. She was in touch with her brother after I took her into my confidence. The reply says Ortega is a rancher out by Backsight and a man of some influence in the town."

"If he'd that much influence he wouldn't bother trying to scare you off," Dusty answered. "He'd just tell the land agent not to sell and make sure he didn't."

"And it doesn't sit right that this Ortega *hombre* would know how to organize these tries on you in Louisville and Nashville," Mark went on.

"I thought some about that too," Raines admitted. "It all ties in with this Ortega though. There's nobody in the East would want us not to go."

"What new folks are there on the train, folks you haven't known a fair time at least?" asked Dusty.

"Very few. Miss Considine, she's the land agent's sister and joined up with us in Nashville. A young woman called Simons joined us there too."

"Why not ride back to the train with us, Dusty," Louise inquired, seeing how worried her father looked.

Dusty glanced at the sun. Soon it would be dark and there were things he wanted to attend to before joining the train.

"We'll head back to Hammerlock and see what's to be

learned. Happen we're lucky we'll be out with you at around ten o'clock. Like I said, we'll ride along with you and Lon'll take over as your scout."

With that Raines had to be contented for the three young Texans were clearly determined to go ahead with their plans. Raines knew the risks they were running, that they would be facing odds of seven to three. He also knew they knew the risks and the odds, accepting both with their quiet confidence in Dusty Fog's planning to bring them through. He mounted his horse and nodded to Louise to do the same.

"We'll expect you then," Raines said.

"We'll be there, Colonel," Dusty promised.

It was dark when Dusty, Mark and the Kid entered a small livery barn in the town. It was not the establishment they gave their trade to but a smaller and not so well cared for building at the other side of the town. They were walking along the row of stalls and looking at the horses when the owner came from his office.

"Hey!" he growled advancing in a belligerent manner. "What's the idea. You can't come in he—"

Mark turned, towering over the bleary-eyed and unshaven man. "Just set real easy, mister. We're interested in that light bay hoss. Who might own it?"

"Says which?" growled the owner although he looked a mite uncertain.

"Wouldn't belong to our ole friend Cultus Collins now, would it?" Dusty asked.

"You don't need to answer, just waggle your ears happen we called it right," the Kid went on, taking out his bowie knife and absently paring down his fingernails with the razor-sharp edge.

"It belonged to him all right," gulped the owner.

He'd taken in the spread of Mark's shoulders, the cold, hard-eyed look of the Kid and the dangerous way the smaller man stood. He knew this was no longer the time for loyalty to one's customers.

"Been hard run today, hasn't it?" the Kid went on.

"I wouldn't know."

"What sort of rifle does Collins tote?" Mark inquired.

"Why'n't you ask—"

The words ended in a startled yelp as Mark's hands clamped on the man's dirty shirt and lifted him clear from his feet. "I'm asking you!"

"He's got a Sharps but he didn't have it when—"

The man stopped for he remembered Collins giving a grim warning to say nothing about the ride he took that afternoon and from which he returned on a lathered horse which had been run hard.

"That his Sharps in the office?" Dusty asked.

"Nope, mine. He'd got his with him, unloaded it here. I took the empty case into the office to reload it for myself."

"Go fetch it here," Dusty ordered. "Then tell us where we can find Mr. Collins."

CHAPTER FOUR

Red Blaze Joins In

THE young Texan that Mark Counter claimed to be the notorious Red Blaze watched Louise charge to her father's defense, but did not follow. Moving back around a corner, he watched the subsequent scene with a sad grin. After Louise and the men departed he emerged and leaned on the hitching rail until Collins' bunch came from the saloon. When they walked by, Red followed at a distance.

After walking a short distance, Collins' party halted and looked down a side alley. Saying something to the others, Collins walked down the alley and his men swung around to block its entrance. Being unable to follow Collins without attracting unwanted attention, Red waited until the man returned. Collins led his men off once more and Red darted down the alley, but could find no trace of who, or what, attracted the hardcase's attention. Walking back to the street, Red saw Collins' crowd enter Saloon Ten. He decided to see if whoever contacted Collins in the alley showed again. So a few minutes later he slouched into the saloon with hat shoved back, hair rumpled and untidy and a loose-lipped, drunken grin on his face.

On unsteady legs Red made his way across the room to the bar, ignoring the suspicious looks thrown at him by the men with Collins.

"Gimme a bottle, mister," he told the bartender, his voice whisky lined. Fumbling in his pockets Red hauled out a handful of change and dumped it on the bar, poking out the price of the drink in an owlish manner. He yawned and eyed the bartender. "I'm a tired cowhand 'n' a long ways from home. Just want a place to sit down 'n' rest. Un'erstand?"

The bartender nodded in understanding. He was something of an authority on the habit of drunks. His right eye lowered in a wink as he set a bottle of whisky on the counter and topped it with a four-finger glass. The cowhand crossed the room in a waving and uncertain manner as Collins called for drinks. Flopping down at a side table Red started to sing a cowhand song in a muddled way, then his head fell forward on to his arms and he lay as if asleep. Collins threw a glance at the redhead, then ignored him as being of no importance, just a cowhand sleeping off a drink.

Time went by and the bartender lit his lamps as the darkness came down outside. One of Collins' men left the building on some errand and after a time came back fast, face flushed from running.

"They're here," he said.

"Where?" asked Collins.

"Down to the livery barn and likely to be coming here."

One of the other men looked toward Collins and asked, "You're sure you didn't cut down that scout, Cultus?"

"I told you I didn't," Collins answered. "I just wanted you boys to side when I tried to muscle in and get the chore."

"All right then, we'll back you in it."

The bartender gulped. He could read the signs and knew his place might see some trouble real soon. His hand went under the counter and felt the comforting butt of the Wells Fargo ten gauge, while his eyes went to the redhead who appeared to be asleep still.

Collins stood up, shoving his chair back. The hand which held his glass shook slightly, for he was sweating and scared. The three Texans were looking for him; they must know something. His only hope was to start shooting as soon as they entered the saloon. One shot would be enough and the men with him would be forced to back him up whether they wanted to or not.

The bearded man was at the window looking out. He turned with a scared look on his face.

"They're coming, Cultus, near on here."

Boot heels thudded on the sidewalk. The Texans must have come unseen by the lookout along the other side of the street and were crossing. There would be little or no time to organize a defense.

"Fan out, boys," Collins croaked. "Get—"

The redhead came to his feet, hands curling back and lifting his Colts clear as the thumbs drew back the hammers. The double click was echoed by the gentle words of warning.

"Stand fast and live long, gents!"

Collins looked in the bar mirror, seeing the way the Texan stood. One thing was for sure, he was not drunk and had not been from the moment he entered the room. With an angry snarl Collins tensed to take action.

"Like the gent says," growled the bartender and slapped the ten gauge on the bar top. "I ain't having my fittings busted up."

The footsteps halted by the door so the men outside could see in without showing themselves.

"Come ahead, Cousin Dusty," called the redhead. "They're all hawg-tied down and plumb peaceable."

The batwing doors opened and Dusty Fog came in, moving forward. Mark Counter followed, stepping to the right then the Kid joined them prowling to the left and looking as mean as all hell.

"Leather your guns, Cousin Red," Dusty drawled. "Thanks for your help, bartender."

"I just didn't want me bar wrecked," the bartender replied and replaced his shotgun beneath the counter.

"Enjoy your ride this afternoon, Collins?" asked Mark Counter.

"Ride?"

"Ride," agreed Mark. "With a hoss. You know how and what I mean."

"I wasn't out on my hoss today." Collins answered and his bunch gave rather unconvincing grunts of agreement.

"We know you did," Dusty put in.

"You got proof he done it?" asked the man who spoke to Collins just before Dusty's arrival.

"We've got proof."

The man looked at Collins. "We said we'd help you scare that dude into taking you on as a wagon scout, Cultus. I liked you up to a point but you passed that point if you murdered a man to get the job."

Collins stared at the men, seeing they were all in the same frame of mind. "I didn't kill Tom Blade!" he yelled. "Get them!"

With that Collins sent his hand down toward the butt of his remaining Starr gun. Dusty Fog's right hand crossed his body, came back with a Colt in it. The Army Colt bucked in Dusty's hand even before Collins completed his draw and the stocky man spun around, crashing into the bar with a bullet-broken shoulder.

"Don't shoot!" he screamed, clinging to the bar. "Don't kill me!"

"You dropped Tom Blade," Dusty replied quietly, his Colt cocking again.

The other men stood fast for they were under the guns of Dusty's friends. Mark had thrown down on the men the same instant Dusty made his draw and the long-barreled Colts were in his hands only a flicker behind Dusty's shot. Red Blaze was also armed—having beaten the Kid to it, although neither could really claim to be fast—using the lined weight of his Colts to help Mark persuade a lack of movement from the men. The Kid's old Dragoon was covering the bearded man by the window, ending his move as surely as when they first met.

Collins rolled his eyes in fear and pain as he faced Dusty Fog. He was holding his shoulder and moaning as blood ran between his fingers.

"Who'd you see down the alley, Collins?" asked Red Blaze.

None of the men saw the side door of the building open slightly. Then the Kid saw Hammer's eyes flicker to it. The Kid glanced and went into action with the speed of his Comanche blood.

"Look out, Dusty!" he roared and the old Dragoon boomed like a cannon in the confines of the room.

Several things happened all in seconds. The roar of the Kid's Dragoon echoed and drowned out the crack of a shot from the barrel of the revolver which showed around the edge of the door. Flame lanced from the barrel and Collins jerked, then slid down, a hole in his temple, the other side of his head shattered where the bullet came out once more. Dusty went to one side, twisting to face the door with his Colt ready. The man called Hammer saw his chance, for the Kid's attention was on the door. Hammer went through the window, carrying glass and sash with him. His rapidly departing feet were echoed by the sound of someone running away from the side door.

The Kid hurled across the room to the batwing doors but he was too late, for the bearded man was not in sight by the time he reached the street. Holding his Dragoon ready the Kid sprinted to the corner of the building and flung himself around it into the shadows at the side. The alley by the saloon side was empty; whoever killed Collins did not wait around.

Calling a warning the Kid went to the door of the building and opened it. He looked at the hole his bullet made, opening the door, then glanced down, but as he expected the iron-hard ground outside showed no sign.

In the saloon Dusty came to his feet and snapped, "Hold them down, Mark, Red. I want to look into this."

With that he walked to the door and looked at the hole left by the Kid's bullet, while he tried to gauge how high the killer's revolver was held. One thing was for sure, shooting like that was not done from waist high. The revolver was sighted before it fired and sent the ball through Collins' head.

"About this high," drawled the Kid, pointing to the place where the gun was held. "I'm near on sure of that."

Dusty looked at the hole made by the Kid's Dragoon. On the exit side, a large chunk of wood had been blasted out and with luck might have caught the killer, for it was not on the ground. He estimated the killer stood at least five-foot-six and maybe more, there was no way to check. Dusty was almost sure he heard a yelp of pain just after the shot but could not be certain. Likely the splinter hit flesh and not the bullet, for nobody went far carrying the round lead ball of a Dragoon in the body.

The Kid made another search along the wall and to the rear of the saloon, he came back with a piece of wood in his hand. It fitted to the splintered portion and on the tip of it was blood. Beyond that there was nothing at all to find and no sign which might tell him what kind of person the killer might be.

"Let's get back inside," suggested Dusty.

The five men who backed Collins looked uneasy as Dusty and the Kid returned. The one who'd done all the talking so far spoke up.

"Look, Cap'n," he said. "We weren't in on no killing with Cultus. Knew him from way back and I said we'd help him to shake down a job of scout on a wagon train. That was when he came in a few days back. This afternoon he rode out, told us he was after seeing the wagon master and we didn't have cause to disbelieve him. He come back and allowed they wouldn't take him on. Then when Hooks Hammer, him that lit out through the window, told us the wagon master had just rode in we thought we could throw a scare into him and make him take Cultus on. We didn't even know the scout was dead."

"These boys have been around town for some time now, Cap'n," put in the bartender. "And Collins only rode in a couple of days back."

The gunman threw a grateful look in the bartender's direction. "That's true. Cultus allowed he was doing a riding job for somebody but didn't say who. We sure wouldn't have backed him had we known he'd killed a man."

There was nothing in the man's expression which might show he was lying and Dusty was inclined to believe him.

"Who did this *hombre* see when he went down that alley back there?" asked Red, stepping forward.

"I don't know. We heard this voice call to Cultus, was sorta muffled like the speaker didn't want to be known. He asked us to make sure nobody came down the alley and went along it. We never saw who it was and all he said was that it was his boss."

Again there was nothing against this being the truth. Red knew none of the other men went down the alley with Collins and likely couldn't have seen what happened at the other end.

"What now, Dusty?" he asked.

"Depends. Where's the town law, bartender?"

"Out to his house, about three miles down the Bisbee trail, allows the night air's bad for him."

"He could be right at that," drawled Dusty, glancing at the broken window. "That'll take some fixing."

"Sure," agreed the bartender bitterly, for his saloon was not the best patronized in town and the repairs would wipe out most of his week's profit.

"Hammer was with you bunch." Dusty remarked, eyeing the gunmen. "Was I asked I'd say you should pay for the repairs."

The five men exchanged glances but did not argue. They dipped their hands into pockets and forked out enough money to cover the repair of the window, then leave a bit over. The bartender grinned out his gratitude as he scooped the money into his cash drawer.

"Now drift," drawled Dusty.

The men went with signs of obvious relief. Red Blaze watched them go and then swung to face Dusty.

"Why'n't you hold them?" he asked.

"In a town where the law spends its time three miles outside?" replied Dusty. "What'd be the use of that?"

Dusty looked down at the body on the floor. Tom Blade's killer was dead, Dusty was sure of that. Now it remained to get the man or men behind the killing. There was more to Tom's death than an attempt to take over the scout's job; it did not pay well enough to warrant such action. More, there was the shot which wrote finish to Collins. That shot, fired to stop him talking, meant the killer's boss was on hand.

"You didn't need that Sharps bullet after all," remarked the Kid. "And I don't see why you ever did."

"Aimed to show it to Collins and say we found it at those rocks, see if I could trick him into making a mistake," Dusty explained, then looked at Red. "How did you come into this?"

"Was doing like you said, watching the other street, for the first sight of old Tom, when this gal come along and got into a fuss. I helped her out, found who she was and started to bring her to you. When I saw you head this bunch off I set to and followed them. I didn't figure it'd come to Tom being killed but reckoned you'd want to know where they went. Then I thought whoever called Collins down the alley might show up again, so hung on."

"You did the right thing," Dusty stated.

"For once," agreed the Kid. "Say, what'd you tell that gal? She was like to walk all over us."

"Didn't tell nothing but the truth," grinned Red.

"It should happen to you one day," growled Mark. "Did you learn anything out there, Dusty?"

"Nothing much at all."

"From what I saw it looked like a thirty-six caliber gun," remarked the Kid.

"Which same's what I thought," agreed Dusty. "Tolerable fair shooting at that. Just a quick aim, one shot and Collins wasn't talking any more. It's time we were gone. Tend to him for us, bartender."

The man behind the bar nodded. Collins had been sporting a fair roll of money which would more than cover the cost of his burying. He watched the Texans leave the saloon and came around to attend to fetching the local undertaker.

"Not much notice taken of the shooting," Mark remarked as they walked along the street. "Nobody seems bothered one way or another."

"A bad town," was Dusty's reply. "It'll change, fact being it'll have to change when Backsight grows."

"Say, that Hammer *hombre* might have headed to the livery barn to collect his hoss," growled the Kid.

"It's not likely," replied Dusty. "He'll hole up somewhere until he knows we've left town. I'm more interested in who left the train and came into town."

They collected their gear from the hotel at which they'd stayed while waiting for the wagon train. Then, collecting their horses they rode out of the town. There was no interest shown in their going as there had been none in their arrival. They left the town where the law spent its nights well outside, where a man died and no thought was given to him by the citizens. That was Hammerlock and the Texans were well pleased to be clear of it.

The fires of the wagon train showed up well in the night and the four Texans headed toward them. They saw the train's stock held to one side and turned their horses in that direction. The guard was not asleep and a challenge rang out in the darkness.

"Captain Fog and party," Mark called with a grin at the others.

A big shape loomed up astride a horse and nursing a

Spencer rifle. His voice was respectful as he peered toward Dusty.

"The Colonel allowed you'd be along, Captain," he said. "I'm Jim Lourde, was the Colonel's sergeant-major in the War."

"Jim Lourde, of Chickamunga?" said Dusty. "I'm pleased to meet you, Jim."

Lourde took the hand which was held out to him. The four Texans shook hands with the man who gained some fame by rescuing wounded under fire at the Battle of Chickamunga. The war was not mentioned again though for Lourde pointed to the circle of wagons and the gathering around the large fire in the center.

"Meeting going on," he remarked. "There's some worried by who's going to ride scout now Tom's gone. I'd have liked to be there but I always ride herd this near a town, keep the sentries on their feet."

"Many folks gone into town?" asked Dusty.

"None that I know of. Of course them who keep their horse by the wagons could go without my knowing."

That was more than likely, Dusty thought. He told the others to leave their horses and walk the rest of the way in. They attended to the big stallions first, then shouldered their saddles and headed for the wagons. Lourde rode with them and showed Dusty the Raines' wagons. The Texans left their saddles under the Raines' living wagon and then headed for the group by the fire.

There was nothing unusual about the meeting around the fire. It was a tradition on wagon trains that any matter of general interest be discussed at night and around the fire. There everyone who wished could stand up and speak, make a point and have it answered. The business of the train would be settled in the hearing of all, any decision made at the fire must be abided by.

A big burly man dressed in the usual manner of a bullwhacker was on his feet and in the center of attention as he spoke in a loud voice:

"I don't reckon we should take some kid for a scout. He's likely not even dry behind the ears yet."

The crowd's attention faded and died away as the four Texans came into the light of the fire and headed for Colonel Raines, who stood with his daughter to one side of the speaker.

"Who're you?" growled the bull-whacker.

The Ysabel Kid moved forward until he stood before the man. His face was a hard cold Comanche mask as he looked the bull-whacker up and down.

"Feel behind my ears, *hombre*," the Kid said quietly, yet his words carried around the crowd.

"What?"

"You're not that deaf. Feel behind my ears."

The bull-whacker's scowl deepened as he dropped his eyes to examine the Kid's dress and armament. "Are you the Ysabel Kid?"

"If I'm not my mammy carried the wrong papoose for months. Feel at my ears."

The bull-whacker was a big, hard and tough man, but knew he was matched against someone just as hard, tough and even more dangerous. The Kid's hands were at his sides but that meant nothing. He could get to his Dragoon gun easy enough. Then the bull-whacker saw the bowie knife and read the signs right. It would be to that razor-edged fighting tool the Kid's hand would flash if trouble began and the Kid would not waste time in fist fighting. If the bull-whacker started anything he would need to push it through to the end and the end would be death for one of them. Slowly his hand lifted and felt at the Kid's ears, then dropped to his side again.

"Wet or dry?" asked the Kid.

"Dry."

"Say it louder. You spoke up loud enough before."

"Dry!" repeated the bull-whacker in a voice which carried around the circle of watching and listening people. With an angry scowl he turned and walked to where four more of his kind squatted on their heels.

Raines moved forward to stand by the side of the Kid. "We've heard what Bull Gantry had to say," he announced. "Now I'd like you to hear what the Ysabel Kid says. He'll ride scout in Tom's place. I also want you to meet Captain Dusty Fog and Mark Counter. I propose to hand over the duties of wagon master to Captain Fog for the rest of the trip."

There was a rumble of talk that went up through the crowd at the words. Every eye was on the small man who had become a legend in his own time. One of the men let out a rebel war yell which others took up.

"That's good enough for us," someone whooped. "We'll follow Cap'n Fog like we followed you, Colonel."

"Reckon you ought to hear what Miss Considine's got to say when she wakes up," growled the man called Bull Gantry.

A tall, well-dressed woman came through the crowd. She was a beautiful and elegant woman, almost five-foot, ten inches tall with blond hair pulled back in a severe way and a face which looked cold and haughty. Her riding habit was rumpled but revealed a plump yet hard-fleshed figure.

"I'm awake, Colonel," she said in a husky contralto voice. "Are these the men you intend to take as scouts?"

"They are."

"They look young for such a responsible position," Miss Considine went on, blue eyes going to Dusty, Mark and the Kid for Red had drawn back from the fire at the first sign of possible trouble to watch the crowd without being noticed.

"I've been troubled by that ever since I was born, ma'am," drawled the Kid. "But took all together we're one tolerable old man."

Miss Considine snorted. "You must remember, Colonel, that we have to reach Backsight and show improvement on our land by the end of the month or title is revoked and the land thrown open for resale by your default."

"I know that, ma'am," agreed Raines. "So do all these others, which is why we're putting Captain Fog in command. They know more about this business than I and so I leave it to them."

"Do they know the way to Backsight?" she asked.

"Never been out that way afore, ma'am," Dusty admitted. "But we know a lil mite about finding our way about and the Colonel's likely got good maps."

"That I have," said Raines. "Tom was using them, for he'd not been to Backsight either. Does that satisfy you?"

"I go along with the majority," Miss Considine replied.

"Do you aim to use this pass through the mountains that Gantry's been telling us about, Captain?" asked a man.

"I don't know until the Kid's looked it over," Dusty replied.

"Gantry allows it'll cut three or four days off the journey," said another of the travelers. "We was wondering—"

"I'll tell you as soon as I know," Dusty replied firmly. "Now I reckon we'd all best try and get some sleep."

The crowd had it laid before them. They could see Dusty didn't aim to be forced into a decision he might regret later and they did not press the matter. It was decided they would follow the route Tom Blade laid down until an investigation of the pass could be made. The meeting broke up and the travelers made for their family fires.

"Did you learn anything in town, Dusty?" asked Louise eagerly. "I mean about—!" The words ended as she saw Red Blaze standing to one side. "You!"

"Me," agreed Red with a grin.

"But Mark and the Kid told me—" Louise began, then stopped as she saw the grins on the Texan faces.

"Red's my cousin," Dusty explained. "He was watching the other street. Fact being Lon'd just come from him when we tangled with Collins."

"Then he's not a—a—"

"Whatever these bunch told you's likely all lies," Red remarked.

Louise swung to face Mark and the Kid, who looked remarkably unashamed at the way they libeled Red.

"You unmitigated pair of scoundrels!" she gasped but

there was a twinkle in her eyes. "I'll get my revenge, see if I don't."

"Man!" breathed the Kid. "Did you hear what she called us, Mark. You want to remember that and call it ole Jimmo back to the OD Connected."

Louise wondered how she could get her own back on the two cowhands. She was aware that they liked and accepted her or they would never have played the joke on her. She knew they would like her even better if she turned the tables on them.

"Hey, Louise," called a voice and Maisie Simons came over carrying a large and freshly baked apple pie. "Yen made this, I wonder if your friends would like it!"

Louise caught the eager gleams in the eyes of the four Texans and took the pie from Maisie. They headed for the Raines wagon and the girl carefully sliced the pie in two pieces handing one to Red and giving the other to Dusty.

"Hey!" yelled the Kid. "Where's ours?"

There was a triumphant gleam in Louise's eyes as she grimly warned, "This's only the beginning."

"What's all this about, Louise?" asked Maisie. "I brought the pie for all four of your friends."

Louise explained the reason for her discrimination and at the end of it the Kid and Mark found they now had two enemies.

Mark caught Dusty's sign and knew his pard wanted to have a chance to talk undisturbed with Colonel Raines. He was about to draw the others clear when Dusty looked at Maisie.

"I didn't see you around the fire, ma'am."

"No," Maisie answered. "I was asleep in my wagon. I think the ride was more than usual today, I don't usually fall asleep like that."

Dusty nodded then turned to Raines. Mark knew this was his sign and started the others off talking by telling a completely false story of Red on a coon hunt. Red yelled his fury at the lie and brought up one of his own about Mark which kept Maisie and Louise laughing.

Pulling to one side Dusty told Raines all that happened in Hammerlock and they discussed the killing of Collins.

"And you think somebody on the train was working with Collins?" asked Raines.

"It looks more than likely. Had we more time I'd send Red and Mark back along your train to ask around and find out if Collins was in any other town you passed. He might have been following you and just waiting his time to hit."

"Why wait until now?"

"This'd be as good a place as any," Dusty replied. "Hammerlock's the last chance for him and his pard on the train to have a definite meeting point. There'd be no way whoever's on the train could be sure of the route Tom'd lead you across the range. But he could be sure you'd go by Hammerlock as the last stop before the open country to Backsight."

"He could even be sure we would skirt that prairie-dog village across the stream too," Raines put in thoughtfully. "Which narrowed his chance of missing us."

"I thought of that," drawled Dusty. "Then there's another thing. Most any other place along your route there'd be lawmen who'd go right into a killing. Not at Hammerlock, there's not that kind of law in Hammerlock. The last thing is that out beyond Hammerlock you could be lost or delayed or stopped the easiest."

"Who do you think killed Collins?"

"I don't even start to know, Colonel. It was a thirty-six gun and whoever used it was a tolerable fair shot. Right now I reckon we should try and get some sleep, we'll be rolling out early comes the morning."

The four Texans spread their bedrolls under the second of the Raines' wagons and Red looked across the circle to where Maisie Simons was climbing into her wheeled home.

"Nice gal that," Mark drawled. "Been around some, I'd say."

"Sure," agreed the Kid. "She's a mite too free and easy for an Eastern widder-woman. It's a real pity I'll be riding scout. I bet she bakes a mean biscuit."

"I'm more interested in how her boots got so dirty," Dusty put in, for Maisie had been dressed in a blouse, divided skirt and high-heeled riding boots. "Her having been in the wagon and asleep. She doesn't look like the kind of woman who'd go to bed, or even doze off, without she'd cleaned up her gear for the next day."

"You're only guessing," said the Kid, although he knew Dusty never made wild guesses. "Maybe she was too tired to bother about cleaning them."

"I'd go with you on that," drawled Red. "Only I saw her while you was talking at the big fire. She came in from the range, leading a hoss."

CHAPTER FIVE

The Gap

"WHERE'S LON?" asked Louise Raines as she came from the wagon in the first light of dawn.

Dusty, Mark and Red stood by the wagon's fire, holding plates of food in their hands, eating with the ease of men who were long used to taking their meals in such a manner.

"Lit out a piece back," replied Dusty. "Come and eat."

She walked forward and accepted a plate of eggs and bacon from the fat, smiling Negress. Already her father was supervising the morning movement, and the drivers were harnessing teams ready to roll. Louise realized that she must have been very tired the previous night, for she was usually up before the harnessing began.

"Where did he go?" she went on.

"Someplace the pie gets shared out fair," Mark put in.

"You poor little man," scoffed Louise. "Did the nasty cook miss you when she shared out the pie. Well, she can always start to miss a few more people too."

"I quit," Dusty answered, raising one hand in a gesture of surrender. "We had the maps out earlier, afore certain folks were awake. So I sent Lon and Jim Lourde out to scout that gap we've heard so much about."

"When will they be back?"

"I told them to try and make it by tomorrow night at the latest," Dusty replied. "That's when we'll have to know, so as we can turn either to the gap or up and around the tip of the hills, whichever's needed."

The men handed their plates to the Negress, who called "Will you-all hurry, Missy Louise. Otherwise I ain't going to have time to wash plates afore we moves out."

Dusty turned to his two companions and gave his orders. "Take a point, Red, Mark. Follow the route we picked and make sure of the easiest going. Find a place for us to camp tonight, then check in and let me know."

"Yo!" came the cavalry reply from the two Texans as they turned to obey.

Louise watched them go with a guilty flush coming to her cheeks as she saw they'd saddled her horse and brought it in with their own mounts. She watched them swing into their saddles and Mark raised his hand in a mocking salute to her, while Red reached down and drew the Spencer carbine from his saddleboot.

All around was the bustle as the people of the train prepared for another day's movement. They were now used to this living on wheels and there was little confusion or time wasted. Louise finished her breakfast, swallowed down the cup of coffee Dusty brought her, then joined him as he went around the train to check that all was ready to roll.

People greeted Dusty, eyeing him with some interest and wondering if this small man could really be the famous Dusty Fog whose lightning raids shook the regular officers of the Union Army. Dusty looked them over in passing, noting that all their wagons were in good condition and that the harnesses were of good leather. The entire train showed care and attention, which pleased Dusty.

A man loading his wagon glanced at Dusty and then looked down to what he was doing. The small Texan came to a halt for he had a good memory for faces and knew the man.

"Howdy, Thad—" he began.

The man turned; he was tall, slim and his hands looked very powerful. He wore glasses and there was a worried look on his face.

"The name's Cauldon, Captain," he said. "Grant Cauldon."

"My mistake, Mr. Cauldon," Dusty answered without a change of expression. He knew he was making no mistake and knew why the man did not want his real name to be mentioned. "All set to roll?"

"Set and ready," the man who called himself Cauldon replied.

"Do you know Grant Cauldon, Dusty?" Louise asked.

"Nope, what's he do?"

"He's a gunsmith and a good one. He's taking rifles and ammunition to sell in his place at Backsight but I've never seen him fire a gun," the girl replied. "I was in his wagon to have papa's Henry repaired and there was one of the new Sharps rifles with a telescope fastened on the barrel. I asked him if he ever used it but he said he didn't and meant to sell it."

Dusty was listening to the girl but he was also watching everything that happened. This was a new experience to him, acting as wagon master, but he had a fair knowledge of mass movement of another kind. The people knew what they were doing and needed no help or orders from him.

It was at that moment Dusty saw a group of men approaching. His eyes took in their appearance, knowing them for what they were and their purpose in coming. They were led by a burly bull-whacker, one of the bunch Gantry gathered with and a man a good six inches taller than Dusty, with broad shoulders and a powerful frame. The others with this bull-whacker were young, brash youngsters from the train, all hot and eager to see how tough this new wagon master was. Dusty knew their kind, knew it and had handled it in the army, as a lawman and as a trail boss. Gantry's pard was not of that kind. He was a frontier hardcase, a bully and on the prod or Dusty did not know the signs.

"They allow you're the new wagon master," the bull-whacker growled.

"So they tell me," came Dusty's soft drawled reply.

"And you intend to go around instead of through that gap in the hills?"

"Likely," replied Dusty, glancing at Gantry who stood behind the other men. "Are you all set to roll, Mr. Gantry?"

"Fred here wants to talk to you first," Gantry replied. "He's been out this way afore and knows the country."

"You'd best listen to me, small man," Fred went on.

"Get to your wagons and ready to roll," drawled Dusty, starting to turn from the bull-whacker called Fred.

The man shot out a big hand, gripped Dusty by the arm ready to turn him around, at the same moment drawing back his other fist. Louise screamed half in fear and half as a warning but she did not need to bother.

Even as the man's hand touched his sleeve Dusty was turning, coming around faster than Fred pulled. Before the bull-whacker knew what was happening Dusty came around and struck savagely. He did not strike in a way any of the men ever saw before; his fist was not clenched. Dusty's driving right hand was flat, the fingers tight together, the thumb bent across the palm and the palm facing upwards. It looked an awkward way to strike to the eyes of men used to fist fighting in the normal manner. For all that Fred would long give profane testimony to how effective the method was. The fingers stabbed into Fred's solar plexus like the point of a bowie knife sinking deep. Fred felt as if the pole of a Texas bellybuster gate latch slipped from his fingers and rammed him in the middle as he leaned from his saddle to open the gate. The bellybuster was aptly named, as Fred knew from experience and those fingers ramming into his body brought exactly the same sensation.

Croaking in pain Fred doubled over, his clenched fist and just-started punch melting in midair. Instantly Dusty hit again, bringing his hand up and then slashing down without changing the way he held his fingers, only this time it was the edge of the hand which landed. The heel of the palm drove into the side of Fred's neck and the man went down limp and helpless as a back-broke rabbit. Dusty bent, took hold of Fred's collar and heaved, almost tearing the man from his shirt as he was brought erect. Dusty released his hold then smashed his other hand across, using a conventional fist this time but hitting with the back of it. Fred's head snapped over and he pitched to one side sprawling on the ground without a move.

Dusty spun to face the other men, his face hard and set, his hands still held clenched.

"Who wants it next?" he asked.

Louise gasped. This was a new Dusty to her eyes, one she'd not seen before. He was suddenly hard, tough and very dangerous. Then she saw the way the brash young men looked at him and remembered how they'd caused trouble with Tom Blade until he handled one of them roughly and gained their respect. They showed Dusty that same respect now.

"Get to your wagons and ready to roll," Dusty barked when there were no takers to his challenge. People were staring from their wagons or places of work, wondering just what happened, for the attack began and ended so quickly. "Gantry, get this *hombre* on his feet, pay him off and tell him that if I see him around the train in three hours I'll send him on his way myself."

Gantry nodded. It was the code of the train. Fred knew the chance he was taking when he said he would show the others how to handle Dusty Fog. The man failed in his try and Dusty was well within his rights in firing Fred. Gantry moved to obey but he wondered how such a small man could beat a tough hardcase like Fred with so little trouble.

The answer was to be found in the Rio Hondo country where dwelled a small, slit-eyed, smiling man. Tommy Okasi, Ole Devil's servant, was thought to be Chinese but claimed his homeland was Japan. The small Oriental knew certain methods of fighting with the empty hand which were almost uncanny to Western eyes. To Dusty Fog alone of the Fog, Hardin and Blaze boys did Tommy Okasi teach the techniques of jiu-jitsu and karate. This was the secret of how Dusty could handle and defeat much bigger and stronger men. His use of the *hiranukite*, the level piercing hand and the *tegantana* or handsword on Fred proved how well he learned the oriental tricks.

Gantry hauled Fred to his feet and helped him toward the wagons. The bull-whacker made no attempt to go back and resume the fight. Dusty didn't think he would. So Dusty turned and headed for the Raines' wagon, where the Colonel waited with a mouthful of questions about what had happened.

"Let's roll, Colonel," drawled Dusty before the same questions could be asked. "Start them out."

The first wagon was barely moving when Miss Considine rode up on a big and powerful-looking horse. She brought the horse to a stop, glared at Dusty, then turned her attention to Raines.

"I must protest about this assault on my driver, Colonel!" she snapped.

"I did the assaulting, ma'am," Dusty put in. "Protest to me."

"He came to you with a matter of some importance—"

"He came looking for a showdown and got one, ma'am," Dusty corrected. "Last night around the fire was when he should have made his play and talked his talk, not this morning after I gave the order to roll. He knew it and knew what to expect. The way he pulled me round I thought he aimed to hit me. I could be wrong about that; happen I find out I am, I'll apologize, if I ever meet him again."

"I agree with Captain Fog," Raines stated. "Last night at the fire he told us what we would do and that was when your man should have argued. He broke the rules and got what he asked for. I saw it all and I thought he meant to try and attack Captain Fog."

Miss Considine looked from one to the other. There was anger in her eyes as she turned the horse and headed back along the line of wagons. Dusty watched her for a moment then swung back to Raines.

"Thanks for backing me, Colonel," he said.

"That's what I'm here for. I always get the impression, watching Miss Considine, that she's not as new to this wagon life as she makes out."

"How do you mean?" asked Dusty, watching the wagons draw by, then looking to where Fred, slouched in his saddle, rode away from the train.

"Just little things. The way she never made any of the mistakes the other women did when they first started out. Then in the desert country she never once forgot to shake out her boots in the morning before putting them on. She did it even before Tom Blade warned us about it."

Dusty thought about his. It was an elementary precaution, shaking out one's boots before putting them on in desert country. Scorpions were likely to crawl into the boots in the darkness and could inflict a nasty sting if trodden on. The Simons wagon rolled by at that moment, driven by one of Maisie's Chinese helpers. Maisie raised her hand in a friendly wave as she passed, calling a greeting. Dusty watched her wagon, thinking of the way she and her helpers prepared to move. Of course, the journey had been long enough for them to learn the best and fastest way to work but there was an air of competence about them which seemed to speak of more than this one trip's knowledge. The previous night there had been no reason for Maisie to lie about not being at the fire, for it was voluntary and nobody need attend unless they wished. There was no reason why Maisie should not take a ride either across the range or into Hammerlock. Dusty could think of even less reason why she lied. He wished there had been time to send the Kid in a circle to check on the tracks leading from the train to the town. However, time was a thing Dusty found himself fresh out of. The gap through the hills must be scouted so the puzzling questions went unanswered. One thing Dusty did know. Both Maisie and Miss Considine would bear considerable watching.

The Ysabel Kid and Jim Lourde rode toward the foothills and the gap leading through. Lourde found time to marvel afresh at the way the Kid, without the aid of map or compass, found his directions across this completely new country. Lourde carried both map and compass but the Kid laughed when shown them.

"You're traveling with a Comanche, Jim," he said. "We traveled this land afore you palefaces came and didn't have maps or compasses."

With the inborn skill of his Indian forefathers, the Kid found his way. He would ride to the top of a high point, sit his big white stallion as he checked the range ahead, then lead Lourde unerringly to the next high point and always in the right direction. Lourde insisted on checking his map first but after the second check called it off, for the Kid was more accurate than the map.

They'd made a cold camp the previous night, no fire, no coffee, just stream water and jerked beef. The latter was beef which had been sun dried for easy carrying and much prized by the Western traveler for its nourishment, if not for pleasant aroma and appearance.

Bringing his horse to a halt, the Kid pointed toward the ground. His Indian-keen eyes were constantly on the alert, checking the range ahead for his directions, searching for sign of ambush and checking the ground close up for tracks. He dropped from the saddle to examine faint marks which attracted his attention.

"What is it, Kid?" asked Lourde.

"Hoss tracks."

"Apaches."

"Not unless they've took to using shod horses. This's the track of one man, afork a shod horse. He went through here about eight hours back."

"Who might it be?" inquired Lourde.

"Might be anybody, there's a tolerable lot of folks in the West that I ain't met yet," replied the Kid with a grin. "The sign's not plain enough for me to tell much more than its age. Might be a soldier riding despatch. Could be a cowhand headed West to look for a fresh job."

The Kid did not mention the other possibility which occurred to him. The tracks were in near enough a straight line with the town of Hammerlock. The bearded man who made his escape when Collins died would have about eight hours' start. It could be him, more so if Colonel Raines guessed right and the killing of Tom Blade tied in with somebody in Backsight.

The tracks headed straight toward the gap which showed in the line of hills ahead. Riding forward once more the two men studied this gap with interest, it was wide enough to allow a Conestoga wagon passage. What caused it neither knew, although Lourde guessed at some ancient earthquake splitting a crack through the hills. On either side of the bottom of the track, the walls rose steep at this point, but there was room, even if not much to spare, for the large Conestoga wagons to roll through.

Studying the conditions of the trail, the width of the track and the way the walls rose up on either side, the Kid and Lourde rode a fast lope. The gap was not straight nor were the walls steep and sheer all the time. There were winding curves, sharper turns around which a Conestoga would need careful nursing if it was to avoid getting stuck. Sometimes there were places in which two wagons might run alongside each other, but these showed rarely and never for any length. Most of the way one wagon could move, even though it might rub against the sides. In other places rocks lay in the track and these would have to be moved before the wagons came by.

"What do you reckon, Kid?" asked Lourde.

"Take more'n a day to come through here. There's no water or graze for the stock. You'd have to camp stretched out in line like this at night. Happen there are Apaches about they'd never have a better chance of making a hit than here. They could pitch rocks down and wipe us out."

"You don't like it then?"

"Less 'n' less all the time. There's something bad wrong

about the entire thing, Jim. No wagon train ever come through here."

"Gantry allowed he'd come through it," Lourde pointed out.

"Yeah. I reckon we'll ask him about it when we make the train again."

They turned a sharp corner and came into a part of the gap where the slopes were not so sheer as in other places. The trail between the walls was wide enough for one wagon in comfort—except for the huge rock which blocked it.

The Kid stopped his horse and looked at the huge slab of rock. It would take long hours to smash the rock with sledge hammers and picks. His eyes went from the rock to the slopes then looked at Lourde.

"That settles it, Jim. We don't come through here."

Lourde was also studying the rock. It lay almost fifty yards along this long and open stretch and to his eyes presented little or no problem. Already his mind worked out where to lay the charges of gunpowder which would blast the rock into pieces. He did not look up at the slopes and so failed to notice the loose shale. The Kid had seen and read the danger from the same shale.

"Why the fast decision?" Lourde inquired. "We could blow that lump out of the way easy enough."

"Happen you stop to think about it, Jim, it's tolerable strange nobody ever come this way with wagons before. Folks from the back country moving down to Hammerlock to buy supplies, the cavalry shipping provisions to the outlying forts. Nobody ever tried to use this gap. You thought of what'd happen if the train was stopped in here and couldn't get no further on?"

"You're way out of my sight now, Kid. I just don't follow you at all."

The Kid swung down from his saddle and reached for the blanket roll which hung strapped to the cantle. For this journey he did not carry his full roll, having left the suggans and his warbag with the Raines' wagons. Wrapped in the tarp was the one blanket he deemed necessary for comfort, a package of jerky, his powder flask, bag of ready-moulded .44 balls for his Dragoon and a box of flat-nosed .44 Winchester rimfire bullets for his rifle. He lifted out the powder flask, one of the old kind made of cowhorn scraped so thin the level of the powder could be seen through it and with a measure fitted to the top, giving him the correct forty grain load for his old Dragoon at every turn of the lever. Checking the level of the powder the Kid turned to Lourde.

"Reckon you could spare some loose powder, Jim?"

"Sure. I'll let you have some combustible cartridges if you like."

The Kid grinned broadly. "Not for me. I pour her in raw and put a round ball on top happen I want to shoot something."

With that he took a handkerchief from his Levi's pocket, opened it, spread it on the ground and tipped some of his powder into the center, then returned the horn to his bedroll which went behind the cantle again.

"Just pour a pit of powder on here, Jim," he said.

Taking out his powder flask, Lourde poured some of its contents on to the small pile in the center of the handkerchief. The Kid gathered and knotted the four corners of the handkerchief, then set it on a small protuberance of the rock. Mounting their horses, without the Kid explaining his actions, they rode back to the corner. Rounding it, the Kid dismounted and drew his rifle.

Watching the Kid line his rifle, Lourde wondered how he hoped to shatter the rock with such a small amount of powder. Before Lourde could raise the question, the Winchester cracked, throwing back echoes which merged with the deeper boom as the powder, struck by the bullet, exploded. Instantly there came a dull rumbling and to Lourde's amazed eyes it seemed that the walls of the gap began to move as shale started sliding down to block the trail.

For minutes it seemd like a nightmare. The echoes of the shot and explosion clashed with the rumbling of moving rock, slamming back and forward along the gap. Only by an effort did Lourde manage to control his spooked horse, but the Kid's white stallion stood like a statue even when a large rock crashed down and narrowly missed it.

The two men stood looking back to where the explosion took place. The big rock was no longer in sight, being buried by the shale which came sliding down from the slopes above. The Kid nodded, for he'd expected nothing less. Turning he jumped over the rock which almost crushed him in its fall, walked forward and vaulted afork his old Nigger horse.

"What'd have happened had she blown when the wagons were in here, Jim?"

Lourde was not an imaginative man but he could almost picture the scene. The wagons halted with no way of moving the fall of rock ahead of them, not in the time they needed to reach their new home and make the necessary improvements on the land. There was more to it than just that, Lourde saw as he rode back through the gap. With no way to turn the wagons they each would have to be eased out backwards, no easy task for the rear wheels had no steering play. Days it would take, weeks more likely, and all that time without water or food other than that which could be hauled in.

There was still more to the picture, Lourde saw as they rode back toward the entrance to the gap. The rock which came down so near him did not fall alone. Other pieces were dislodged by the explosion, they lay scattered along the trail. Any wagon which found itself struck by such a rock would have been damaged beyond any repair and helped delay the retreat still further.

"One thing's for sure," drawled the Kid. "We won't be using this gap now."

They were riding through the entrance and on to the open range once more and Lourde turned in his saddle to look at the narrow opening.

"I wonder if—" he began. "Naw. He couldn't have known about it."

"Who?" asked the Kid, although he could have guessed.

"Gantry. He was so all-fired set on having us come up this way?"

"Tell you, Jim," replied the Kid with a grin. "I don't aim to sit out here and think about it. Ole Dusty gets all riled up too quick for liking happen he's kept waiting. I reckon his mammy spoiled him when he was a button, way he takes on."

With that the Kid started his big white stallion forward, heading across the range. With his Indian sense of direction to help him he aimed straight for a point where he would most likely find the wagon train or some sign of its passing.

Camp had been made for the night when the Kid and Lourde arrived, and a good-sized crowd gathered at the Raines' wagon to hear the news.

"How about it, Lon?" Dusty asked, seeing Raines and his daughter come out of the wagon and join the crowd.

"Waal, to start with the gap's there. Kind of narrow in places but there. Fact being there's places where it gets so narrow the wagons'd scrape the paint off their sides getting through."

"But they could get through?" asked Miss Considine from the front of the crowd.

"Likely they could, ma'am," agreed the Kid, watching the woman and the bull-whackers who drove for her. "Only it'd take two or three days at least and no food or water for the stock through it."

Lourde watched the Kid and wondered what he was playing at. Knowing the way things stood at the gap, Lourde could see no sense in building up hopes. However, he said nothing and allowed the Kid to play things the way he saw them.

"We could carry water and food as we did in the desert country," Maisie Simons put in. "We can still use the gap?"

"No, ma'am," answered the Kid gently.

"No?" Miss Considine snorted. "What's this all about, Mr. Lourde?"

"The gap's blocked by a rock fall," Lourde replied.

"Which same'd take more'n a month to clear, happen

we'd got enough men and the right gear, which we ain't. Even without the chance of another fall while they clear the first," the Kid went on.

All the time the Kid watched the faces of the crowd, reading the disappointment on most of them. He could read nothing on either Maisie or Miss Considine's face and decided that if either could play poker he did not aim to tangle in a game with them.

"We can't go through then, Lon?" asked Dusty.

"Nope."

"After seeing it I'm not sure we could have got through even without the rock fall," Lourde went on. "I thought you said you'd been through there, Gantry?"

Gantry's face showed a look of injured innocence, the sort of look a man might show if he tried to do a good deed and had it slapped back into his face.

"Me? I said I'd heard about it from an army scout who'd been through. He allowed a wagon train could go through."

"One thing's for sure," drawled the Kid. "It wouldn't get through now."

The crowd broke up. They were disappointed that the promised shortcut did not present itself but there was nothing they could do about it. Lourde headed for his wagon while the Colonel's servants brought food and coffee for the Kid. Louise sat beside Dusty and looked the Kid over.

"I smell a rat," she said.

"Where at's Mark and Red?" the Kid drawled, ignoring the girl's suspicious looks. "Their hosses weren't around."

"I sent them up ahead as scouts," Dusty replied. "They'll be back soon. Now tell me about the gap."

"Like I said, it's blocked," replied the Kid, innocent as a newborn babe.

"When did it get blocked?" asked Dusty, knowing his dark friend real well. "Just recent?"

"You might say that," agreed the Kid and told Dusty all that happened.

Raines leaned forward the better to hear every word, his cigar sending up smoke into the air. He made no comment and at the end, while the Kid ate, Dusty turned to the Colonel.

"What title do you hold your land under, Colonel?"

"The usual. Payment of half the price as a deposit to be forfeit if I and the others don't make good on the contract clauses about arrival and improvement of the land under a certain date. There's plenty of time."

"But there wouldn't have been happen you were stuck in that gap for as long as Lon allows you would."

"Then you mean the agent and his sister are in on this scheme to stop us making the deadline?" demanded Raines, throwing an angry look in the direction of the Considine wagons. He looked ready to rush down there and throw the woman and her drivers in irons for the rest of the trip.

"I didn't say so, although it's possible," Dusty replied. "It could be some outside bunch trying to stop you and knowing suspicion would easily fall on Miss Considine. You know how high land speculation runs in the East, Colonel."

"Happens me, Red 'n' Mark takes Gantry out there alone and talks some to him we'd come up with some smart answered questions," drawled the Kid.

Dusty threw the Indian-dark young man a cold stare. The Kid looked more innocent than a dozen choirboys headed for church but he was quite willing to do just what he suggested. He was capable of using a certain inventive spirit to augment the ancient tortures used by his Comanche forefathers to make Gantry squeal if not talk.

"That'd do no good. Happen you're wrong you've got trouble for damaging an innocent man. If it's right there'll still be no real proof and we've tipped our hands that we suspect Miss Considine. Sure there're a lot of things pointing to it being her. Maybe there's too much. Folks with as much at stake as there is behind this wouldn't stop at throwing suspicion on somebody else. They haven't stopped at murder and they wouldn't have stopped at getting us stuck in that gap, so they aren't stopping at a little thing like getting an innocent woman in bad. If it is an outside bunch they'd have ways of finding out who was on the train, of getting their men hired in the right place, to the land agent's sister."

"The only other person in the train who isn't known to us or to the others is Maisie," Louise put in coldly when Dusty stopped speaking.

"I've thought about that, too," answered Dusty. "Have you ever been in her wagon?"

"I have," said Louise and the coldness was even more in evidence.

"Does she have a gun?"

"I've seen a Mississippi rifle and a shotgun, that's all. She's my friend and I trust her."

"Bad Bill Langley's my cousin and I trust him," the Kid put in, "but there's a tolerable lot of folks who don't."

"That's not the same thing at all," snorted Louise, wondering if the Kid was joking about the notorious Texas gunfighter being his cousin.

"Pull your horns in, gal," warned the Kid. "I can't help the sort of kin I've got. There's some of them aren't so all-fired keen on me since I started working cattle in daylight and paying duty on gear I take into Mexico."

"Let's concern ourselves with the local barbarians, not the Ysabel family," suggested Louise, her good temper restored.

"Look at it this way, Louise, gal," Dusty went on. "She's your friend. But happen she was working for some outside bunch, who'd it be better for her to make friends with?"

Louise was forced to admit the truth of the words. She knew what Red said on the night outside Hammerlock and wished Dusty would allow her to ask Maisie if she'd been into town. Louise hated the suspicion which gnawed at her and wanted to clear Maisie as a friend or know her as an enemy.

Before there could be any further discussion Mark and Red returned from their scout. They took their double-girthed saddles to the wagon and Red drew something from inside his saddleboot before he followed Mark toward the fire.

"How's the gap, Lon?" asked Mark as he came up. "Say, Louise, how about some coffee for the hard workers?"

"No good," drawled the Kid. "That's to both questions. What's up ahead?"

"One steep grade that'll take some hauling over about three days on," Mark replied. "Then beyond it rolling, easy country as far as we could see, not going beyond the grade. Looks like there's plenty of water, graze and easy driving."

"Sure, there's nothing much to worry about at all," agreed Red.

Something in the way Mark and Red spoke made Louise watch them more carefully. In the time since they'd come together, the girl had grown to know these Texas men pretty well. There was a grim note under the promise of easy driving up to and beyond the one bad slope. Dusty also knew this, knew it better than did the girl. He waited for Mark or Red to carry on with their report.

"We should make some good time for the three days to the slope," Mark went on. "Likely spend a day hauling up it, it's that bad. Then we could look to easy running for the rest of the trip likely."

"Except for?" asked Dusty.

"This!"

Red lifted his left hand, bringing it and the thing he'd held concealed at his side up into view. Every eye went to the thing he held out into the light of the lamp which the old Negress set on the folding table ready to serve supper.

It was a long, thin stick with feathers at one end, a bright steel barbed point at the other and bands of color painted in the middle. Louise stared at it for a long moment, sudden cold fear gripped her and she gasped:

"It's an Indian arrow!"

CHAPTER SIX

The Slope

FOR a moment after Louise identified the object Red Blaze held out there was silence. Then the Kid laid down his plate and took the arrow from Red, turning it over between his fingers.

"That's only one part of it, gal. Like looking at the cartridge case for a specially made rifle and saying it was a bullet. Where'd you find this, Red?"

"About ten mile ahead," replied Red. "Was luck I found it, I reckon. Laid on the ground under a mesquite bush."

"And?"

"Like I said, it was laying under this bush pointing toward the middle."

"How close was the point to the bush?" asked the Kid, looking just a trifle relieved at the words.

"Maybe four or five inches."

"It was only an arrow some Indian dropped," Louise objected. "I don't—"

"Put, not dropped, gal," interrupted the Kid. "No Injun's going to be careless enough to lose an arrow like this one.

Look at the flights. They're best picked and matched goose feathers. The shaft's arrow weed, chosen specially for its straightness and the same thickness all through. These bands of color now, they're the lodge and wickiup sign of the brave who owned the arrow. That head. It's steel, good steel and sharpened up careful. This's a war arrow gal, been laying out maybe two, maybe three, days, might even be more, there's not much damp in the air to rust it. And it was put, not dropped under bush. How big a bush was it I mean compared with the others that were around, Red?"

"Middle-sized," Red answered, for he knew something of Indians himself and knew the vital need for accurate information.

"Which same means a middle-sized camp out there, maybe four or five mile from where the arrow was left. Arrow tip points to the bush which means head for the camp, happen you're a bronco bad hat Apache and looking for more of your kind to join with. It's a war arrow, so that means there's war medicine being made. Gal, we've got us some Injun trouble likely."

"But if the arrow is calling the men to camp we should be all right," the girl replied.

"Might be, mostly likely might not, knowing Apaches. Some old man chief's calling for men and not so's he can make talk. He aims to put on the paint, or as you Virginia dudes call it, prepare for war."

The situation was not so grim that Louise forgot to plan revenge on the Kid for his remark. She did not have time to speak for Raines was on his feet having tossed his cigar to one side.

"Against us?" he asked.

"Maybe, Colonel, maybe not," replied the Kid. "I've seen no Apache sign and I don't reckon Mark or Red have, apart from this arrow. Like I say, some old man chief's made his medicine and it come out war. He's gathering in men to prove his medicine. Happen they have luck on smaller places they might hit at the train."

Dusty made his decision. "Louise, get around the train

and tell the folks I want to see them all. Colonel, have your servants make up the fire in the center ready for the meeting. Ask Mandy there to throw the Kid some food together; he's riding as soon as he speaks to the folks. Do you want Mark or Red along, Lon?"

"Nope. I'll ride alone and I'll go Injun style, without saddle and take two of the Colonel's blood hosses with me. I want something that'll have the legs of any Apache war pony, happen I get lucky and find their camp."

Raines had a bunch of good horses, the nucleus of what he hoped would be a fine stock. He planned to run a horse ranch out by Backsight but knew the Kid's need was greater than his own. There would be no need of the horses if the Apaches were to wipe out the train.

"I'll pull out come midnight," the Kid remarked when permission was granted. "Be back when I know something."

Dusty nodded. He left such matters to the Kid for there was no man who the small Texan would rather have ahead as his scout. If the Apaches were out in force the Kid would find them and get back word in time for the wagon's defense to be organized properly.

The people were gathering around the big fire in the center of the camp by the time Dusty and his friends finished eating. Then he went forward and stood in the center, a small man but every eye was on him. The brash young trouble-causers of the train were troublesome no longer. They'd seen what happened to a big man who crossed Dusty's path and knew here stood their master. The other men remembered Dusty's name from the War and knew he was their leader.

Dusty wasted no time as soon as he saw every family and all the drivers were on hand. He told of Red's discovery and of what the Kid made of it. He warned them of the possibility of an Apache attack and went on:

"There are two things we can do. Wait here and send a rider to Hammerlock to telegraph the army for a cavalry escort. The nearest cavalry's at Fort Becket, a week's ride from here. There'll be delays before they move and even then we may not get the escort. That's the first choice. The second is we move on, closed up and ready to fight. Which do you want?"

The crowd fell silent, for this was a vital decision for them to make. They remembered all they'd heard of the Apaches, the most savage of the fighting Indian tribes. They weighed this against the delay waiting for possible army help would cost. It was a small but important fact that the cavalry would wear the hated Union blue when they came and no self-respecting Johnny Reb wanted to think he was taking a favor from a Yankee. There was the thought that the delay might cost them their new homes and the money they spent on the deposits.

Jim Lourde stepped forward. "If you say we move on then we move, Cap'n Fog. Apaches or no Apaches, we'll follow your orders."

There was a yell of agreement from the listening men. Captain Fog, the hero of the Confederate Army, the master of light cavalry tactics, the raider whose name stood as high as did John Singleton Mosby's or Turner Ashby's, would be able to match and beat any Apache ever born. The drivers, the hardy bull-whackers, other than Miss Considine's trio, gave their approval, for they were hardy men and paid to do a job. They'd fought Indians before and did not think the Apaches would be any greater danger.

With the matter settled, Dusty called the Kid forward. Standing in the flickering flames, looking savage as any Indian himself, the Kid gave forth of his inborn knowledge of such matters. He warned of the dangers of straggling or straying any distance away from the main body. The Apache was a master at the art of concealment and would lay for hours patiently watching and waiting for a chance to snap up an unsuspecting white victim. The travelers must cling together, hunting parties staying as parties and never less than four men along, preferably with a repeating rifle for added protection. The hunting parties were to be organized, the flanks and rear guarded by pairs of outriders, not single men. If one of the pair was to be shot by Apaches the other must leave him and head back to warn the train. There must be no staying to help the shot outrider; the train was more important.

The Kid also laid stress on the Apache's habit of hitting at dawn when the guards were tired. There was little chance of a full-scale attack at night for the Apache did not fight in the darkness. He would sneak in to try and steal horses or cattle though and so all guards would need to be on the alert. The Kid suggested every dog in the train be allowed to either roam free all night or be fastened outside of the wagons to give an extra warning.

The crowd listened, even though many of them were much older than the Kid. They were hearing words of wisdom from a man who knew Indians from A to izzard and who would steer them through if he could. Their lives, the lives of every man, woman and child on the train depended on following the advice of the tall, slim and Indian-dark young Texan with the babyishly innocent face and the cold, red-hazel eyes.

It was an alert, though not nervous or panic-stricken camp that night. The sentries were never more alert but without having their trigger fingers ready to throw lead into shadows or at innocent noises. The Kid left at midnight, riding one of the best horses Raines owned, using a saddle blanket and no saddle. He led a second fine horse and his big white followed him. Dusty watched the Kid ride, saw him go as he had so many times before, riding into what could be either death or something to which death would be preferable. Dusty did not allow himself to brood or think about it. The Kid knew the risks he took, took them wide eyed and openly, as did every member of Ole Devil's floating outfit when they rode upon a chore.

The train rolled out at the crack of dawn and although Louise was hoping to discuss the likelihood of Maisie's guilt with Dusty she never was given a chance. Dusty rode at the point of the train with her father and kept her on the move, riding with messages to the flanks, the rear guard or to any wagon which tended to lag and make a gap in the train. It was her own fault she mused, as she changed her horse for the third time. She asked Dusty to give her work and he was doing just that.

Red ranged ahead of the train, always in sight, for Dusty was firm on that and far behind them alone, save for his matched Army Colts and his Winchester, was Mark, watching their backtrail for the first sign of the Apaches.

It was around two o'clock in the morning that the Kid returned, on the second day of his journey from the train. He came in silence and Dusty, not a heavy sleeper at such times, did not wake up until the Kid was almost to him. For all that there was no slow transition, no half-awake stirrings and mumblings. Dusty came from fast asleep to completely awake in a flash, rolling from his blankets and holding his Army Colts in his hands.

"Easy, *amigo*, it's me," drawled the Kid.

It took a man with cool nerves to ignore the fact that he was covered by guns in the hands of three men who could call their shots, for Red and Mark were also awake. The Kid never even batted an eyelid, for he knew none of his friends was the kind to throw his shots without knowing where they were going and for what purpose.

The Raines fire had died down but the Kid drew wood from the rawhide "possum belly" under the wagon and got the blaze rising again. The old colored woman peered out of the wagon where she and Louise bunked at night. She saw the four young Texans gather around the fire and climbed from the wagon to make coffee for them.

"We've got trouble, Dusty," said the Kid.

"That figures. You wouldn't have been back if we hadn't."

"I found their camp easy enough. It's some bigger than we expected. Likely got more men joining all the time. The braves are out, split into bunches of between ten and thirty to test out the medicine. There's maybe two or three hundred of them at the camp now. One of them same bunches knows about the train."

"You sure of it?" asked Red. "I never saw any Injun sign."

"One of their scouts saw you. Now they's laying up about a mile over the top of that steep grade and they're not waiting for the planting moon so's they can put down their crops," drawled the Kid, then grinned at the worried looking Red. "Don't get all into a mucksweat, Red. That scout wasn't no green button fresh from off the hoss herding. He was a brave grown and knew what he was doing. You'd have had to ride two more miles at least afore you found any sign of him and been real lucky if you found it for he didn't leave much. I wouldn't have found it but I *was* lucky and using the same route he took earlier."

The other three knew how much, or little, luck was involved. The Kid not only thought but almost was an Indian when he rode scout. That he and the Apache each selected the same route took little explaining. It was the route which offered the best concealment and easiest travel to a man who did not wish to be seen.

"Then they aim to hit us as we go up the slope," Mark put in. "We should be able to hold off a bunch that size."

"If there's only a small bunch now. I saw signs that the war medicine's been lucky enough for them to try and take on something big. Anyways, Apaches are no man's fools. They wouldn't stack thirty braves against a train this size. Way I see it they're camped a fair piece back and waiting for the train to be moving up that slope. Then they'll hit it. If there's a small bunch they'll wreck what they can, scatter the remuda and stock. If it's a big enough branch it'll be like the Alamo all over again, only a damned sight messier."

The old Negress poured out coffee, hardly understanding half of what was being said. She handed around the cups and waited to hear if that Cap'n Fog wanted anything more. The old woman watched Dusty with a smile flickering on her face. There was a man, she thought, a real big man.

Dusty was aware of his responsibilities to the people of

the train. Even now they could run back to the comparative safety of Hammerlock and hope for an army escort. That would be the safe and easy way of a prudent man. It might cost these people all their worldly goods, cause them to lose their homes but save their lives. He knew the decision was his and his alone. He could call on Colonel Raines as leader of the train, or even put the matter to a vote, then whatever happened would see him in the clear. He could have done either but that was never Dusty Fog's way. If the responsibility of wagon master called for a decision then he would make that decision, stand by it and push it to the bitter end.

"This slope'll be about a day's drive, I reckon," he said.

"Near as, damn it," agreed the Kid. "You'd likely get there and stop for the night by a fair stream that runs along the bottom, then haul up with fresh teams the next morning. Which same'd be when the Apaches aim to hit you."

"Make me a map of the area if you can," Dusty ordered. "Show me roughly how steep the slope is. Cousin Red, go wake Colonel Raines. Mark, shake out Jim Lourde. Get the maps while you're with the Colonel, Cousin Red."

The two cowhands went fast and without asking questions. They knew Dusty of old, knew he did not expect a man to stand around and talk when that grim note came to his voice.

Raines and Jim Lourde arrived with the speed of old campaigners, men long used to urgent calls in the middle of the night. Raines spread his map on the table while the Kid, with the aid of his trusted old bowie knife, made marks on the ground which told Dusty much, although the Kid never took a formal geography lesson in his life. At least five minutes Dusty stood by the Kid, asking questions, pointing to the map, while the others waited, drinking coffee and watching him. Raines, a full colonel in the War, stood back with the others. He knew how to give orders and how to take them. Here was a man who was his master in a matter of strategy and the Colonel was willing to admit it.

By the time the Kid finished answering, Dusty possessed

a fair knowledge of how the ground at the slope looked. He turned to the others and the two cowhands at least knew he was ready to give orders and make plans.

"Who're the best four drivers on the train?" he asked.

Lourde rattled off three names then paused. He appeared to be hesitating before mentioning the fourth name. At last he went on. "Gantry's about the best driver of them all."

"Get him and the other three. Try not to disturb the camp. I don't want a flock of folks here."

The four men came back with Lourde, clearly puzzled at being shaken out of their rest at this hour of the night. Gantry was particularly puzzled, for he knew his standing with Dusty was not high on account of his earlier behavior. It came as something of a surprise when Dusty passed him a cup of coffee.

"How much spare harness do you have, Jim?" Dusty asked. "Enough to make a double harness for four teams?"

"I reckon so," Lourde replied and saw the angry gleam which came into Dusty's eyes. It was the look of a tough army officer when a subordinate gave a half-answer to an important question. "Yes, sir, Cap'n. There's more than enough."

"Then I want the folks shaking out early comes the first sight of morning. I want an easy run without tiring the teams too much. In the afternoon, Lon, you take out the four drivers here and show them that slope. It's what the Apaches would expect us to do. Make sure they know every inch of it. You drivers look it over, be sure that you know the best route to run a double team up it—in the dark."

"That slope's tolerable steep, Cap'n," Gantry put in. "I've been out this way on hossback and seen it once. I'd say what you want can't be done."

"Which same's going to make it tolerable hard on you, seeing's how you're going to do it tomorrow night," Dusty replied. He did not mention that Gantry was also supposed to have been through the gap in the hills near Hammerlock, for Dusty knew the man was sincere in his desire to help. "I don't know how you aim to do it, but I do know we're going to have to do it just the same."

"Have we any other choice?" asked another of the drivers.

"Sure, turn back for Hammerlock, although we don't know if the Apaches are up all round or not. Our only chance is to run that slope tomorrow night and make sure every wagon's up there by dawn. The Apaches are waiting to jump us as we move up but they won't do it in the dark."

That put the matter down as plain as any of the men would want to see it. They gathered around the marks the Kid made and studied them. This was sort of geography they could all understand, for the average bull-whacker had small use for formal maps. Gantry was telling the truth about the slope, for he had come through this stretch of country, although on horseback. He knew the Kid's sketch of the slope was not far out in its angle. He also knew, as did every other man, just what an Indian attack on such a slope would mean.

"Couldn't we form a circle at the bottom of the slope so they couldn't ride around us, Cap'n?" asked a driver. "Hold them off that way?"

"Nope. We'd be under their guns from the top of the slope unless we stopped so far out that we'd lose the advantage of the cliff anyway. They'd just lay off from us and wait until more of their pards pulled in and they could get us easy. On top and forted up we'll make them think their medicine's gone all bad on them and they'll not be sticking so hard then."

With that Dusty got down to details, giving his orders with clarity and in such a way that the listening men understood them. The men stayed silent, taking in every word Dusty said. He told each of them what his special duty would be, warning that extra plans and changes might need to be made as the situation developed. Mark and Red would each be in charge of a working party, their men selected for size, weight and strength. Raines would be in command at the head of the slope and Jim Lourde at the bottom. The Kid's sole duty was to roam in the night and make sure no

Apache scout sneaked in to disrupt the work. The four drivers would do just that, drive, handle the ribbons of each team as it ran up the slope. Gantry was put in charge of that side of things, being the only one who knew the slope. His duty would be to make sure he picked a route to get them up the slope with as much ease as possible.

"You'll get anything you want by the way of help, Gantry," Dusty said, for the first time letting the chilling "mister" drop when he spoke to the man.

"I want good men at the foot of the slope ready to help with the harnessing, Cap'n," Gantry remarked.

"You'll get them," Dusty replied. "They'd better know that any wagon which isn't up will have to be left. But every wagon'll be to the top and in the circle. We'll have to make sure of that."

The men asked questions, made their suggestions and observations. There was some good natured banter among the deadly serious talk and a feeling of trust built itself, welded together by the small man from the Rio Hondo, the man called Dusty Fog.

In that moment it became clear why Dusty could make bigger and stronger men obey his will. It was not only that he was chain lightning fast with his matched guns. Nor had it to do with his knowledge of jiu-jitsu and karate which made the bigger men helpless in his hands. Dusty Fog was born with the flair for command, the air of leadership which made other men know he would be the one to follow in time of trouble. It was his ability to think ahead, to plan clearly and yet be ready to change his plans which made Dusty the leader of men he undoubtedly was.

The men broke up their meeting, the drivers and Lourde to catch up on what sleep they could get before roll out in the morning. Mark to make his rounds of the sentries and horseherders, while Dusty, the Kid, Red and Raines stayed at the fire.

"You're putting a lot of trust in Gantry," Raines remarked, taking out a cigar and lighting it.

"Likely sir. He's the best driver of them all and he knows

his own life's at stake as well as ours. He'll be too far gone to turn back when we reach the slope. So he'll have to go on."

"Can we make it?" Raines asked after a few moments.

Dusty did not reply for a long moment. His voice was low, gentle, yet grimly determined when he answered:

"Colonel, happen we get that far we've got to make it."

So the people of the train were stirred from their beds at an earlier hour than was usual. Dusty gathered them around the fire which now blazed in the center of the train and told them their position. He held nothing back, the dangers, their only chance, he told it all. There was no comment, for they'd put themselves in his hands and so were willing to leave it at that. Dusty made sure every man knew where he would be working and under which leader, then told the women what would be expected of them. Only when he was sure that everyone knew their correct place for the night did Dusty allow them to make their breakfast and prepare to roll.

There was no rush about the way they traveled through the day, for Dusty wanted to conserve his teams. It would not be easy that night and tired teams might cause disaster.

Ahead of the train ranged the Kid and Red Blaze, the Kid well ahead. Red in sight all the time. They formed a chain of sight which kept Dusty in touch with the country for miles ahead. They used cowhand trail driving signals when there was anything of note but during the day few signals came. The Apaches set their war medicine on the top of that slope ahead and would not bother with the train until it made the slow and tortuous climb on the following day.

Only the train was not going to wait until the following day.

The Kid returned from his scout in time to collect the four drivers and take them ahead to the slope. They rode up it, noting the grade, picking out in the skilled way of men who knew their jobs the best route for them to take in the night. Each driver gave his opinion, although their views almost matched from the start. In their experienced manner they knew what hazards must be overcome and where they needed the help of the two parties commanded by Mark and Red.

Dusty was determined that the Apaches should believe he meant to spend the night at the foot of the slope. He formed the circle by the wide stream, not even fording it. The women followed his orders and began to prepare their fires while the men tended to their stock.

Like a black dressed ghost the Kid was gone. He went astride his huge white stallion straight up the slope and over the top. There were no shots, no sounds to show that the Apaches were waiting. Time dragged by, the tension could almost be felt as the men ate their meals, then moved toward their groups. Jim Lourde and his boss driver rousted out spare harness and prepared improved ways of fixing it to the big Conestoga wagons. All was ready as the sun went down and threw the camp under the slope into pitch blackness.

The Kid appeared, first on top of the rim, then coming down. He waved his hat around his head to the watching men.

"Get set!" Dusty yelled. "Roll them out! Red get your team up there. Mark move your boys in. Louise, tell Jim Lourde to have his men harnessing."

There was a rush to obey but it came as a disciplined rush without panic or fluster. The first wagon was double-teamed and Gantry sat on the box, his long-thonged whip in his hand. Behind him Lourde and his party, all experienced bull-whackers, hitched a team ahead of the six heavy horses which hauled the second wagon.

Sitting the wagon box Gantry swung his whip and bawled out weird bull-whacker curses. The two teams flung their weights into the harness and started forward, splashing through the stream then forward toward the slope. At first it was easy; then the animals hit the slope and started to fight their way up. At the two steepest points waited Red Blaze and Mark Counter, stripped to the waist and with a party of half a dozen of the biggest and strongest men of the train ready to help the wagons over.

The wagon inched its way up the slope, Red and four of his men flung themselves at the spokes, straining and shoving, doing what they could to ease the strain. The men were to work in teams getting what rest they could in between the wagons crawling up.

At last the wagon's team reached the top, their hooves churning the ground as they sought to drag the wagon the last feet. Then it was on top and Raines stood by to show Gantry where he wanted it.

"Leave plenty of room, Colonel," Dusty called, coming up the slope on his big paint stallion. "I don't want the back of the circle too close to the top. Make sure there's enough room for them all to get in."

Raines nodded and went with the wagon showing Gantry where he wanted it left. The first wagons up would be his own and Raines knew they would be bearing the brunt of the attack very soon. He placed the wagon broadside on to the edge of the slope, the rest would form a circle around it, provided they could all be brought up in time. He could already hear the sounds of the next wagon moving up the slope as he watched a party of women, working under Miss Considine and Mrs. Lourde, stripping off the white canopy to stow it safely under the wagon in the possum belly. The wood from the possum belly was piled at the side to act as a protective barricade. The canopy would burn too easily to be left on its supports where a fire-arrow might strike.

"Reckon they'll hear us, Lon?" asked Dusty as the Kid prepared to pull out for a scout.

"It's not likely," drawled the Kid. "They're all about four mile off and making their magic ready to come on us. Haven't even got any scouts out in case we get lucky, see one and don't come up."

On the slope wagon after wagon rolled slowly up. It was not easy and did not get so with practice. The harnessing of the spare team was done faster but the stock grew tired for it was hard work hauling these wagons up the slope.

Dusty came down and suggested the teams which had been used be held clear of the others so that fresh animals could be used while they lasted. This was done but there were only enough spare draught animals for the first three wagons, then the other teams would need to be used again.

By the time half the Conestogas had gone up, Dusty gave the order for the lighter wagons, the buggies and buckboards to move up. This was classed as woman's work usually for they mostly did the driving of the lighter vehicles. Tonight a man was at the reins and others helped shove from behind.

So it went on through the night. At the bottom fires burned but the top stayed in complete darkness. Meals and coffee were snatched when the working parties could find the time. The teams on the slope came down in pairs, but Mark and Red did not leave their places and Louise took food to them.

The stock was moved up next, except for the harness teams. In the dark men and boys worked to hobble every animal to prevent stampede and panic when the attack came. In this they were lucky, for their cattle were Eastern bossies and not the longhorn of Texas which would never have stood for such an indignity.

There was danger in the work, much danger, particularly for Mark's and Red's groups. If the harness of any team snapped, the animals would be thrown into wild confusion and the wagon's weight would drag them back down the slope again over the pushing men. No amount of human muscle could prevent that happening, certainly not the strength of four men.

However, through the foresight of Jim Lourde and Tom Blade, when they fitted out for the trip, all the leatherwork was of good quality and held under the strain.

Through the night they worked on and below the fires winked out as the women stayed at the top when they came up. The last four wagons were the source of most anxiety to the drivers and the men on the slopes. The teams were tired now every animal weary and exhausted on its legs. Dusty, who had never seemed to be still all the night, came down and sent every man to the places to help Mark's and Red's teams. For all that it did not make matters any better as the last of the train creaked their way up the slope.

Dusty threw glances at the sky, seeing the first lightening. in the east and knowing time was fast running out on them. He saw the last of the wagons with its leg-weary team start forward. Things were going to be close, real close.

On top, by the Raines wagon, Louise and the old Negress laid out bullets for the Henry and Winchester rifles, combustible cartridge packets ready opened, powder flasks and bullet bags. The Kid stood by the wagon peering into the darkness, his old yellow boy in his hands, watching all the time.

"Can't we women go down and help push the wagons?" Louise asked.

"Do what Dusty told you, gal, and don't try thinking for yourself," growled the Kid without taking his eyes from the open range ahead.

Louise opened her mouth then closed it again. At other times she could be talkative and get answers, now things were too serious. She looked around and saw the other women also preparing for the fight which was to come.

It was now a grim race against time. The last wagon crawling slowly up the slope. Inch by inch it crawled upward. Inch by inch that bright glow in the east lifted from the horizon, getting brighter by the minute.

"Push!" Mark roared, throwing his giant strength on to the spokes of the wagon wheel. "Push!"

Then the team was on top, feet churning and sending dirt flying, as with a last surge of human and animal muscle, the wagon rolled after them. The driver sent it forward fast and swung it to block the last gap. Eager female hands were ready to unhitch the team while men waited to attend to them, water then hobble them and let them rest.

Mark joined Dusty, drawing on his shirt. He was sweat soaked, leg weary and feeling as tired as when he rode for twenty-four hours in the drag of a trail herd, tailing up the exhausted steers as they dropped. All through the night he and the equally exhausted-looking Red stayed at their place, never leaving it and helping with each wagon.

"Looks like we made it, Dusty," Mark said, tucking his shirt in.

"Looks like we did," agreed Dusty, watching Red draw his shirt on. "You've done well, real well."

The two Texans could have asked for no greater praise or thanks. They took the coffee Louise brought them, went to the side of the Raines wagon and sat down. Dusty made a circle of the train to see everything was ready. It would soon be light enough for the Apaches to see they'd been tricked. Then there was going to be some hell stirred up around the top of the slope.

"You pair ate yet?" he asked when he returned, satisfied there was nothing more he could do but wait.

"Just now coming," Red replied. "Cousin Dusty, you're the hardest cuss I know, up to and including Uncle Devil and Cousin Betty."

"You're just saying that 'cause it's true," grunted the Kid. "Anyways, Betty Hardin's got him all licked to a frazzle for meanness."

"There's none of the three of them to improve the others," Mark put in.

For all that any of the three speakers would have given his life for Ole Devil Hardin, his granddaughter, Betty, or the Rio Hondo gun wizard who ruled the floating outfit.

Dusty ignored his friends but took the plate of food Louise brought to him. Even while he fed Dusty watched the range. There was no sign of the Apaches and he wondered if they would come. He hoped they would, for if the attack failed now the warriors would hang on the flanks of the train and pick another time to make their attack, a time when the train was less prepared.

Around the train people watched the open land, one thought in every mind. Was the extra work justified? Did they really need to take the chances and tire the stock just to reach the top of the slope before morning?

If the thought worried Dusty as he stood by Raines after finishing his meal, it did not show. In his mind he was satisfied the risk justified itself. They were at the top and waiting for the attack when it came. If it did not, all they were out would be the day they'd need to rest the stock. If they had not climbed the slope in the dark they would be coming up in the daylight when the Apaches hit. Then the chances of survival were not great. It was a calculated risk to ensure the safety of the train and Dusty did not regret any part of it.

The sun rose and the range around the train showed wide, clear—and empty of any sign of Apaches. A woman came to ask for permission to light a fire and make a meal but Dusty shook his head.

"Not yet, ma'am," he said.

Louise watched the woman walk away and saw in it another sign of the trust the people had in the small Texan. They were willing to accept his decisions without argument. She turned back to where the Kid looked across the range and could not resist the chance to get her own back on him.

"Where are they?" she asked.

"Out there, gal," drawled the Kid without looking at her. "Making their medicine afresh to see how they've gone wrong, seeing's how we spoiled their last medicine by coming here in the dark."

"Some prophet," she scoffed, still watching the Kid and not the range ahead. "You're without honor in your country this ti—"

The words died away for suddenly the range ahead was swarming with Apaches. They came from out of the ground almost, or so it seemed to the girl. Squat, dark-skinned half-naked warriors astride fast-racing ponies. They did not wear feathers as she expected, only a head band keeping back their shoulder-long and lank black hair. They wore breech cloths which left their thighs bare, their moccasins came up almost to the knees. Most of them were armed with bows but there were firearms, revolvers and muzzle-loading carbines mostly but with a couple of repeaters. No two looked alike or were armed alike. There was only one thing about them which was alike. All wore paint. They were coming for war. Hurling themselves in a fast and deadly rush straight at the train.

CHAPTER SEVEN

Right Lively for Tame Indians

"THERE'S more than you reckoned, Lon," said Dusty quietly as he took up his Winchester carbine.

"Why, sure, likely called in a couple more bunches," replied the Kid, hefting the yellow boy.

The camp was ready and there was no alarm, only tense expectancy. The men were mostly veterans of the War and used to being faced with an enemy. Mark sprinted to the right of the train, Red heading for the left, while Jim Lourde was to command the side facing the edge of the slope, with orders to stop the Apaches using it as a place to hide their snipers.

Red's drive across the train ended when he slid under a wagon where a pale young man and woman knelt. The man was Red's age but did not fight in the War so was not used to the idea of fighting. He was newly married before leaving the East and his wife knelt by his side loading a Mississippi rifle while he held a second and belted a Leech and Rigdon Navy revolver.

"Don't worry none," Red drawled, casually throwing a

shell into the breech of his Spencer and thumb-cocking the big side hammer. "I'm here—which same's right good cause to worry come to think about it."

The woman looked at Red, wondering what to make of that range country piece of logic. It took her mind off the attack which was what Red meant to do. He gave a piece of advice as the first volley thundered from the train.

"Don't empty them both at once," he said, indicating the rifle and revolver.

Mark came to a halt by the side of the gunsmith's wagon and the man called Cauldon nodded to him. Beside the wagon were several open boxes containing rifles of various kinds and one closed box but Mark did not ask what was in it.

"Looks like the Yankees at Bull Run," drawled Mark.

"I hope they don't fight as well," Cauldon answered.

"They make the Yankees look like beginners," Mark warned. "Are all those guns loaded?"

"Sure."

The words were cut off by the crash of Dusty's first volley. It sounded loud but so far there was no sign of an attack on this side of the train.

Dusty looked at the men lining the wagons and facing the first onrush of the Apaches. He saw that Maisie Simons' wagon was just a little further along the line and her three helpers knelt at the ends with their weapons held, one had a Mississippi rifle, the second a shotgun and the third gripped a meat cleaver. There was no sign of Maisie at either end and this surprised Dusty. He did not think the woman would be the kind to shrink from anything which needed doing, even killing raiding Apaches and risking death herself.

Dusty found no time to worry over Maisie as the line of braves charged closer at every raking stride of their war ponies. Dusty glanced quickly at the grim-faced men who faced the rush. Like the Apaches they held a variety of weapons, mostly Hawkens or Kentucky muzzle-loading rifles but with a few repeaters mixed among them, while every man belted at least one revolver.

"Hold your fire until I give the word!" he yelled.

All too well Dusty knew the value of the first volley at such a time. The rifles, primed by hands unflurried by the excitement and tension of a fight, were less likely to misfire through from too small a powder charge, the ball being placed under instead of on top of the powder, or a second charge being placed on one which already lay in the barrel due to a misfire. These things all happened in the heat of a battle, even with trained veterans. The first volley, carefully loaded and aimed would do damage without fear of any such things happening.

"Hold it!" Dusty's voice cracked out even over the fast-growing thunder of hooves. "Hold it! Don't fire yet!"

Raines thrust the point of his Haiman Brothers saber into the ground and looked to where his daughter stood by the side of the wagon ready to reload the repeaters as the men handed them to her. His eyes went to the Kid who gripped his rifle and selected his target but did not fire. The Kid knew his shot might start others throwing lead and ruin the first volley.

Nearer the Apaches thundered, every brave urging his pony to greater effort in his attempt to be the first to count coup on the hated white-eyes. The ground shook to the sound of the hooves but Dusty still held his fire. He wanted them so close that they would get the full power of the volley.

"Easy now," he told the men. "Make sure of your aim. Line careful and make every shot count—Fire!"

The last word brought a crash of shots and a very creditable volley slashed into the Apache ranks. Several men and horses went down but two of the braves made their feet again and were scooped up behind their lodge brothers to be carried clear.

"Reload!" Dusty roared, bringing his carbine to his shoulder.

The carbine and the two rifles began to crash, backed by the other repeaters along Dusty's section of the train.

The Kid's old yellow boy was like an extension of his arm, the way it operated. It moved, sighted and spewed flame, a brave or a horse went down at every shot for at that range the Kid was hardly likely to miss. Raines and Dusty were also shooting fast, although Dusty gave more attention to the rest of the line than to firing his carbine. The men with the cartridge rifles were also pouring in their shots and the faster reloaders brought their muzzle-loading rifles into play.

The Apache attack split, boiling along the two flanks where Mark and Red ordered volley firing. The crash of shots shattered the air on either side, then a volley from the rear told that Lourde's men were given their concrete task in the fight. Methodically and without a thought as to the rights or wrongs of this action the Kid picked off any brave who was down and showed the slightest sign of rising again.

Then the attack was over and the braves were shredding back to the main body who were now in sight and waiting some three hundred yards from the train. A sporadic burst of cheering rose from the travelers but Dusty stopped it. They'd held the first attack but it counted for little. The remaining Apaches would come in again all the more eager to avenge the killing of their friends and lodge brothers and to show the temporary breaking of their war medicine meant nothing to them.

"They're waiting for something, Dusty," drawled the Kid as he forced bullets through the loading slot of his rifle. "I'm not sure wh—yeah! That's it. Look out there!"

Dusty looked and knew what the Kid meant. From the dust which boiled up in the distance a fair sized bunch were coming to join the attack.

"Make sure everything's ready loaded!" Dusty bellowed. "Red, Mark, Jim, there's another lot coming in."

Red's head emerged from under the wagon like a wood-pecker peeping through a knot hole in a pine tree.

"Ain't they hell!" he whooped. "We haven't but worked halfway through this bunch yet."

"Yah!" Dusty jeered, knowing that their light attitude

would reassure the travelers. "I haven't seen any fighting on your side yet."

Ignoring Red's spluttered and furious reply, Dusty turned back to study the new arrivals. They looked to be about thirty or forty in number and rode fast. He could see even at that distance they were all young braves, hot and eager to show the others how fighting the white-eye brother should be done.

"Way they're coming their medicine was good and they've hit some place," the Kid remarked. "So they'll come right in now and the others'll follow."

The Kid's eyes took in the attacking braves, went to the leader. He stiffened and his face took on the cold, slit-eyed look of a Comanche dog soldier. By his side Louise also watched the new attack. She saw the leader, a squat, half-naked brave riding a good paint horse and waving a war lance. Her eyes went to the thing which was stuck on the end of the lance, something roughly oval in shape and with long black hair streaming out behind it. Then Louise screamed and by her side the Kid's rifle spat out fast shots, his hand a blur as it worked the lever.

From the entire front of the wagons came a ragged volley. The young brave was thrown from his horse, torn almost to doll rags by the hail of lead which came down on him. The lance fell from his hand to the ground. The white woman's head impaled on the point bounced free and rolled under the hooves of the horses which charged after the dead leader's mount.

"Pour it on!" Dusty roared. "Get reloaded."

His carbine spat fast as did the Kid's rifle and the Colonel's Henry. It was a dangerous situation now. The volley had almost all been directed at the young brave with the hideous war trophy. Now the men of the train were allowing their wives to reload as the braves hurled themselves into the attack.

Pale with fear, fighting down the hysteria and sickness which welled up in her, Louise caught Dusty's arm. Her face turned toward him and her voice became a croak:

"Dusty, did you see—"

Dusty pushed her arm from his, thrust the carbine into her hands and snapped, "Load the rifles."

His matched Colts were in his hands, the right lifting and lining then crashing out a shot which tumbled a racing brave from his horse.

The newcomers had taken coups; the white woman's head proved that; their medicine was done up real good for them by their war gods. So they forced home the attack with more determination than had the first party.

Dusty's left-hand Colt bellowed into the face of a brave who was in the act of lining his war bow down. The brave jerked, the arrow snapped down away from his bow string and fell, beating its user to the ground by a matter of seconds. Then Dusty saw something out of the corner of his eye and looked at the Simons wagon.

A young brave was racing his pony in line with the wagons. He'd fired a shot from his carbine and was reloading it, Apache style. First he poured a shot of powder down the barrel, allowed the powder flask to swing back by its thong, slipped a round soft lead ball into the barrel. Lifting the gun he slammed the butt down on to the withers of his pony, doing it hard enough to seat the powder and ball at the bottom of the barrel. He was slipping on a percussion cap when a hand showed from under the Simons wagon. The hand held a Navy Colt with a twelve-inch barrel. It was a white hand, not belonging to one of the Chinese employees. The long barreled Colt kicked once and the young brave went sideways from his horse, not even having slipped the percussion cap on the nipple of his gun.

The hand disappeared even as Dusty watched; it came into view a second after to spit again and tumble another brave at a range that would have taxed the revolver shooting skill of many a man.

Dusty was so interested in the long barreled Navy Colt, although more in the shooting skill than the novelty of it, for he'd seen such weapons before. He heard a yell and twisted around to see an Apache hurling from his horse over the barricade and full at him. Dusty went backward in a dive, the Apache sailed over his head to land with catlike agility. Raines saw this. His rifle was empty, just handed to Louise for reloading. He did not even try to draw the revolver from his holster. His right hand caught the hilt of the Haiman saber, brought it up and across in a slash which laid the Apache's belly wide open and sent him stumbling to his knees and then down on to his face, his intestines spilling from the wound.

Throwing a fast shot into a brave who tried to follow the first, Dusty did not have time to thank the Colonel for his help. He caught the Kid's accusing look and then gave his full attention to the fight. Luckily Louise did not see the full horror of the Colonel's saber stroke and thought her father had only used the point. She forced the bullets into the loading slot of Dusty's carbine with fingers which trembled but did their work.

Under his wagon Red handled his revolver while the girl slipped a copper tube of bullets into the butt magazine of the Spencer. The braves were sweeping along the flanks now, shooting as they rode and wheeled their horses, probing for a weak spot, then turning their horses to charge against it. Sometimes the attacking brave was shot down well clear. Other times he was inside the train before he could be dealt with.

Mark and the mild looking man fired when they saw a target. The man was a very good shot, his rifle work brought more than one brave crashing to the ground. There was a yell from one side of Mark and he turned. Three braves had forced their way into the circle, leaping the barricade between the two Considine wagons. One of Miss Considine's drivers went down under an Apache, knife in his chest. Bull Gantry shot the second but the third was behind him, bringing up his carbine. Mark started to bring around his Colt but he saw Miss Considine, down the line, turn. The woman held a Remington Beals Navy revolver in her right hand. She brought it up and fired fast. The Apache spun around, dropped his carbine then fell. Mark could see the shot was one which called for accurate sighting as the Apache was partially concealed behind Gantry. The third brave was cut down by the big bull-whacker's rifle even as he was about to send an arrow into the women and children who were grouped behind a protective barricade in the center.

Mark's attention was brought back to the fight and he was able to give no thought to Miss Considine's good shooting. It was good shooting, the woman handled her gun like a master and there'd been no flurry or mistake making in the way she sighted then shot down the Apache, killing him instantly.

Red Blaze heard the girl gasp, following the rattlesnake buzz of a ricochet. Turning his head he saw she was bleeding from a gash which ripped her dress sleeve and laid a bloody furrow bare to view.

"Keep shooting!" he growled to the young man. "I'll do what I can!"

One glance told Red the wound was more painful and messy than dangerous but it had been a very close thing. He told the girl to slip back from under the wagon and run to where the doctor was already in business attending to the wounded. He watched the woman go, holding her arm as she wended her way through the churned up dust of the milling livestock which were being kept under control by a party of women told off for the job.

Then Red was shooting once more. He saw a pair of braves close in, one holding a Springfield carbine, the other a bow with an arrow already on the string. He took the bow toter as being the most dangerous and shot accordingly. The brave's face turned into a red mask as the .44 ball hit him and he went backward, his arrow sailing into the air. The second brave threw his Springfield to his shoulder, sighting down on Red. The young man at Red's side brought his revolver up and pressed the trigger, letting the hammer fall on a percussion cap. The Apache gave a scream and came down off his horse, hit under the chin by the .36

bullet and with the top of his skull gone as the bullet came out.

"Keep shooting!" Red growled, seeing the young man's pale face and hearing his gasp as he looked at the bloody shape in the hoof-churned earth outside the train.

It was one thing to pour rifle fire into a racing bunch at a distance and not know for sure if your rifle was doing the killing. It was another thing again to throw a shot into a man close up and know your bullet and your bullet alone was responsible for the taking of a fellow human being's life. It was a hard and bitter lesson but the young man must learn it if he was going to live in the hard frontier land which was Arizona in the late 1860's.

The Apaches drew back again. It was a bloody repulse which cost them many lives and the train only a few. The people in the circle were lucky although lucky was perhaps not the best word. They'd followed Dusty's orders and made good, strong barricades from behind which they could shoot in safety, for the Apache bullets and arrows would not go through.

Quickly Dusty reloaded his Army Colts. Louise turned toward him, her face ashy and pale and her hands shaking.

"Did you s-s-see that—that—"

Laying down his Colts on the table Dusty caught the girl by her shoulders and shook her hard. "Stop it, Louise!" he snapped. "We can't do her any good and being hysterical's not going to help you stop the same thing happening to you and every woman on the train."

"Look at it this way, gal," the Kid went on. "She was dead when they got her, which same's why they did what they did. She was lucky—they might have took her alive."

The girl looked from one Texan to the other. Then her eyes went to her father who stood away from the others and watching the Apaches. She opened her mouth.

"No you don't, Louise," Dusty said before she could speak. "You don't wish you'd stayed home, not just through this. Or if you do I reckon me and the boys have wasted a lot of time and friendship on somebody who wasn't worth it."

"How did you know what I was thinking?" Louise gasped.

"You'll never make a poker player, gal," grinned Dusty. "Not unless you learn to hold that face in better. You didn't even mean it to yourself. Now load those guns ready. We're a long ways from out of the woods."

Louise turned back to the table and carried on loading the rifles. She knew that Dusty was right. This was a testing ground. A woman who came to live on the frontier must be prepared to accept whatever life brought. The fate of the white woman whose head lay out there might be the fate of every woman on the train if they allowed panic to run away with them. Her eyes went to where the Kid now stood by her father.

"Right lively for tame Injuns, Colonel," he drawled. Then he stiffened and stood more erect to peer away into the distance. "You got them field glasses handy, sir?"

"In the box on the table," replied Raines. "I thought you didn't believe in using such things?"

The Kid grinned but would not be drawn into defending his previous scoffing at the use of such artificial aids to long distance viewing. In fact the way he focused the field glasses showed he was not entirely unfamiliar with their use. He stood erect, scanning something out on the range with the glasses and looking very excited. It would only have shown to somebody who knew the Kid but Colonel Raines was one who could tell the difference in the laconic casual way the Kid now stood and his normal posture. Handing the glasses to Raines the Kid turned and went toward Dusty. Raines lifted the glasses and trained them across the range. He could see nothing unusual in the line of braves who sat their horses and waited to attack again. Beyond them were a bunch of women who loaded dead warriors on to horses. That could hardly have interested the Kid, for it was normal Apache behavior; they always tried

to take their dead with them when they went from a fight.
Time after time a brave risked death to swoop down and
carry off a dead or wounded companion during the attack
on the train. There was nothing much more to make the Kid
show much interest, only a very old Indian who sat his
horse on a knoll, holding a rifle over his head and looking
up at the skies.

"We've got us some luck, Dusty," the Kid drawled.
"The leader of this bunch's out there making his medicine.
The old man chief himself trying to find out how come his
war gods done stopped looking with favor on their fair-
haired boy. If we can drop him we'll break the attack and
they'll head home real fast."

"Reckon we could do it?"

"He's almost five hundred yards out and won't come in
any closer. He don't need to. His name's made as a fighting
man, he don't need to take the risks, that gets left to the
young braves just making their names."

"Five hundred yards," mused Dusty. "Not even you
could make a hit at that range with a .44 rimfire."

"I know," agreed the Kid, a calculating gleam in his
eyes. "I figured two or three of us could get afork our hosses
and make a rush, chance fighting through to a range where
I can hit him."

Dusty smiled, a grim cold smile. "I've already passed
the bet on that one. You'd be buzzard bait before you got
twenty yards out and I don't want to wish that even on to
a buzzard. Besides, happen the ole chief sees you coming
he'll know you're after him. It's no go, Lon."

"It'll hold down the attack."

"No!" barked Dusty. "It'd be certain death for whoever
went out there. The only way is for us—hold things here
for a few moments, Lon. Colonel, if he tries to leave the
circle shoot him through the leg. Do it easy, I want him
fit for work when I get him back to the OD Connected."

Dusty went around the circle, using his time to check
on ammunition, powder and other supplies and on the num-
bers dead or wounded. He was satisfied with the results of

his planning and the few casualties. Coming to a halt by Mark's side he looked at the mild man.

"I'd like to borrow that Sharps rifle, Thad."

The man did not reply as he opened the closed box. Inside fitted into grips so that it would be held safe and without humping, lay a Sharps buffalo rifle. It was .45 in caliber and used the Berdan-style bullet. Along the barrel was fastened a black tube, a telescope, making the new type of rifle the most accurate long-range weapon in the world.

For all that Dusty knew the Kid, good shot that he was, could hardly be expected to make a hit at five hundred yards with the first shot of a rifle he'd never handled before. The Kid was used to the open type sights and the telescope would take some mastering. It would need to be a one shot hit for at the first miss the Apache chief would take himself somewhere out of sight and make sure he did not give a second chance.

"We need the rifle now, Thad," Dusty said quietly. "But more than that we need a man who can hit at five hundred yards with it."

"Thad?" Mark put in. Then the light dawned. "You're Thad Baylor, aren't you, friend?"

The man called Cauldon looked from one to the other. By his side his wife was pale, her eyes on her husband's face.

"I am."

"And you never admitted to it?"

"The sort of work I did in the War wasn't what a man wants to boast about," the man replied. "Yours wasn't the only assignment I handled, Captain Fog."

Dusty remembered the sort of work Thad Baylor did in the War. In more modern times he would have been known as a special duty sniper, sent to pick off vital targets. Dusty remembered one time he and Baylor worked together. A Union spy was making for the Union territory with vital information. He was almost six hundred yards away and would soon be in an area where no Confederate troop could go. Thad Baylor was using a captured Berdan Sharps rifle, a weapon not as accurate as the one in the box. For all that Thad Baylor slid from his horse and sighted. His one shot tumbled the spy from his horse, dead without even knowing what hit him. That was the kind of duty Thad Baylor's rifle skill brought him in the War.

"We need that rifle right now, Thad," Dusty put in. "And I need a man who can make the best use of it."

"What do you want doing?"

"There's the old man chief of this bunch sitting out there at five hundred yards he's beyond the range our Winchesters can hit at. If we can drop him the rest won't stay on."

Baylor watched Dusty's face all the time. His voice was low and bitter. "I never wanted to kill. I'm a gunsmith, and a good one. But in the War all I did was kill men. So I changed my name, even after the War the local law kept coming to me. A bad nigger killed two women and hid out in a barn. Fetch Thad Baylor. He'll down him. A hold-up man's hid out behind a tree and shooting down the posse. Got to get Thad Baylor to pull him out of it like a coon off a log. So I changed my name and came west with Colonel Raines. Only you recognized me, Captain."

"This's urgent, Thad, it's got to be done," Dusty answered.

"It always has. Eight times in the War it was urgent. Three times since the Appomattox it was urgent. Eleven men died without knowing what hit them. They were dead as cold pork within seconds of my lining my sights on them."

"And how many folks lived because those eleven died?" Dusty snapped. "That spy you downed. You saved three Confederate regiments at least by killing him. I've seen a hold-up man or two myself and killed them. I've seen possemen, men with wives and kids, killed by some owlhoot hiding behind a tree. If I could have killed the owlhoots the way you did, I would have. I'd have done it to save other men's lives."

"We all did things we didn't like in the War, *amigo*," Mark put in. "This's different. Kill that old man chief and they'll pull out. Let him live and they'll keep hitting us, taking a few more lives each time. You're the only man who can stop it, Thad."

Baylor's wife listened to every word. She knew how her husband felt, knew how he hated the killing the War forced upon him. Yet her eyes went to a woman who was weeping as she stood by her wagon, her husband dead at her feet. Slowly Mrs. Baylor went to the box and took out the rifle. She turned to her husband holding the long gun out.

There was a cold look on Baylor's face as he removed the glasses. They were plain glass for his eyes were just as keen as ever and he only wore them as a disguise. Nobody who remembered Thad Baylor, would take a man who wore glasses all the time for him, the finest shot in the Army of the Confederacy.

"Just one shot?" he asked.

"That's all you'll get," Dusty agreed.

Baylor reached into the box and took out a single brass shell, slipping it into the breech. Then he followed Dusty toward the Raines wagon. He attracted no attention for the other people were attending to the wounded, loading weapons or snatching the brief respite to take a drink or a bit of food. Raines looked surprised when he saw Baylor coming with Dusty, for he knew the secret of the man's identity. There was no time wasted for the braves were getting restless, waiting for the old man chief's medicine to be made.

Climbing into the Raines wagon Baylor rested his rifle on the edge. Dusty gave the Kid rapid orders and the dark young man followed Baylor in, not knowing what it was all about but knowing for sure from Dusty's tones this was not the time to ask about it.

"That's him, right out back," drawled the Kid.

"I've got him," Baylor replied, removing his coat and making a pad of it on the edge of the wagon. "Around five-fifty, I'd say. Just a little wind blowing almost straight at us."

He settled down comfortably, resting his left hand, gripping the foregrip of the rifle, on the coat. His left eye closed and his right focused along the telescope sight. The Kid did not speak; he often jeered when his friends mentioned such a sight but this was too serious a matter for jeering. The Kid's eyes were on the old man chief as Baylor settled down behind his rifle. The warriors were looking back toward their leader, only a few giving any attention to the train. In a few minutes now the medicine would be made and the brave-hearts would go pouring down on the white-eyes, wiping them and their train into a blazing and bloody mess.

Baylor did not rush his aim. The Sharps rifle was the most perfect of its kind but like all black powder weapons likely to be erratic and uncertain at extreme ranges. The slightest breeze needed to be taken into consideration when shooting at a range of over a quarter of a mile.

The rifle boomed out once, black powder swirling over the target as shown through the telescope. For all that Baylor had the instinct of a good shot, which told him he'd made a hit. The Kid, to one side, saw the old man chief suddenly jerk, the rifle falling from his hands. Then he pitched from the horse's back and hit the ground in that limp and boned way a dead man always fell.

"Got him," growled the Kid and grabbed the rifle from Baylor's hands. "A real Tennessee meat-in-the-pot hit!"

At that moment every Apache let out a hideous yell which brought all eyes to them. Around the rank of warriors the wail rose, mournful and wild. Every eye was on their fallen chief and the man who had raced his horse toward the spot. The man looked down, then spread his hands waist high and outward. It was the sign which meant finished—dead. Slowly brave after brave rode forward, away from the train, the dead chief was lifted across his horse and the entire party rode away, the death song droning out as they faded into the distance.

"It's a trick!" Raines spoke the words which were on the minds of the train's people.

"Sure ain't, Colonel," the Kid replied, jumping from the wagon with the Sharps rifle in his hands. "He was the chief who made the medicine and when Tha—I downed him the others knew their medicine was bad. They've pulled out and it'll take days for them to pick out a new old man chief and for him to make his medicine. We'll be long gone from here before that happens."

The words carried to the people at the nearby wagons. It passed on around the train and cheers started while men asked who fired the shot which ended the life of the chief.

"Mr. Cauldon," Dusty barked as Thad Baylor followed the Kid from the wagon. "You can have that rifle back now; thanks for letting the Kid use it."

"Good for you, Kid!" yelled a man and the cry was taken up by others.

Thad Baylor took the rifle and walked back to his own wagon where his wife waited. He could hear men cheering the Kid for the good shot he made. Baylor did not worry. He'd done what he needed to do and nobody suspected he was Thad Baylor of the Confederate Army.

"I hope I never have to use this gun again," Baylor said to Mark as he rested the rifle against the wagon.

"A lot of folks are alive who might have died, because you used it," Mark replied. "Don't you fret none, Mrs. Cauldon, ma'am. Nobody'll connect your husband with who he is. Not through Dusty and my knowing."

Mark raised his hat to the woman, then turned and headed to where Dusty Fog was waiting to give orders for the cleaning up, the removal of the dead Apaches and the burying which must be done.

CHAPTER EIGHT

Red Blaze Meets a Man

THE people of the train let their cheering die away as the Apaches faded from sight. Bull Gantry came along the wagons and halted before Dusty, holding out his hand.

"You called the play right, Cap'n Fog," he said. "If we'd been running up that slope when they hit none of us would have made the top."

"I couldn't have brought the wagons up without good men to drive in the dark," Dusty replied. "Take charge of the stock, will you. Have them run down to the water, let them drink then graze. Keep a guard on them, although I don't reckon we need it now."

The Kid collected his big white and Red's claybank; they saddled and rode out without waiting for orders, following the departed Apaches to make sure they did not return. It was not likely but a man lived longer by not taking fool chances and by not passing up any bets, no matter how unlikely.

Dusty was about to start work when he saw Maisie coming from under her wagon. She put a hand to her head and slid to the ground. A group of women gathered about her and Dusty walked toward them. Maisie lay on the ground and one of the woman looked up at Dusty.

"The poor dear's fainted, no wonder, caught under that wagon all the time."

Dusty did not reply. He saw another woman hurrying forward with a bowl of water in her hands. Dusty gauged his distance, then by a seeming accident tripped the woman, caught her and steadied her but the water flew over Maisie. The result proved what Dusty suspected, for Maisie gave a startled squeal and came out of her faint far quicker than one might have expected. Dusty apologized to the woman for his clumsiness then walked away. He was thoughtful and his thoughts were directed to the young woman called Maisie Simons. He knew she'd shot down at least two Apaches with the long-barreled Navy Colt and did not know why she should pretend to faint like a scared Eastern woman. Her faint was pretended for the recovery had been too fast for it to be otherwise.

The thoughts cut off as Dusty found himself surrounded with people who each wanted his or her particular problem dealt with. The train preacher, a young man whom Dusty liked and admired as being what a man of the church should be, was making his rounds, comforting the bereaved but giving them work to do which would stop them brooding and falling into despondency. The wounded needed care and attention but Doc Fremont had that in hand. Dusty gave his orders; men to dig graves were sent out with Jim Lourde in command. The stock was already heading down the slope. The dead Apaches were removed and Dusty gave Mark a task which brought a wry look to the big man's face. However, Mark did not argue. He took a sack from the Raines' wagon and walked out. Mark did not expect the thing he was looking for to be pleasant and he was not wrong. He got the thing into the sack and took it to where the grave-digging party worked, leaving it to receive Christian burial, which would be more than the rest of the dead woman's body would receive unless the Cavalry found the burnt-out home before the buzzards and coyotes finished the meat and the ants left nothing but a skeleton.

Mark felt sick. In his life, from seventeen, he'd lived with violence and done more than his fair share of killing but the horror of that head was the worst thing he'd ever seen. He walked around the train, watching the boys, with the callousness of the very young, collecting the Apache weapons which lay around. They picked up knives, war axes, lances, pulled arrows from woodwork of the wagons and found bows. Mark went forward to give a warning about touching the firearms discarded or dropped by the Apaches and about fooling with the bows and the razor-sharp, needle-pointed war arrows.

A fight broke out away from Mark. He directed his steps toward it, bending and scooping up two wildly thrashing boys, holding them apart and in midair with a big hand gripping each boy's waistbelt.

"All right, all right, that's enough fighting," he snapped. "Aren't there enough arrows to go around?"

"Not like this'n, Mark," replied one of the boys, delighted that he was one of the two selected for special attention by the big Texan.

Mark glanced at the arrow which lay at his feet and saw straight away what made it so special. Fastened around the shaft was a piece of white paper, and Mark could see the string which fastened the paper to the arrow. He bent and took up the arrow, dropping the two boys onto their feet as he did so.

"I'll take this'n," he said. "Where'd you find it?"

"Over there, on the ground," one of the boys replied, pointing to just in front of Maisie Simons' wagon.

"Now you light out and stop your fooling with those Apache guns," Mark ordered. "Leave them be until the menfolks can collect them."

The boys muttered their disapproval but already Dusty had men going around to collect the firearms and make sure they were unloaded. So the boys headed out in search of more arrows.

"Found this," drawled Mark, holding out the arrow.

Dusty took the arrow and turned it over between his fingers. Before he could speak he saw the Kid and Red return. They joined him with the news that the Apaches showed no signs of returning and that he could discount Apache attack as a factor in the train.

"Good," drawled Dusty. "Where'd this come from, Mark?"

"Near the Simons wagon," Mark replied. "On the ground, the kid who found it told me."

"Fired from an Apache bow?" asked Dusty mildly.

"That's what we're supposed to think."

The Kid grinned. He could use a Comanche buffalo-bow with some skill and knew this arrow never left any kind of bow, not with the message attached to it. The bulky knots by which the paper was fastened were on the side of the arrow which slid across the face of the bow when fired, would have struck it and deflected the arrow.

"No Apache fired this," he drawled. "What's the message?"

Dusty worked the paper free without unfastening the knots, then spread it out open and looked down at the writing.

" 'This should warn you,' " he read, " 'that I mean business. Turn back or the next time the Apaches won't stop.' "

Raines came over at Dusty's call. He took the paper and looked at it, then growled, "I'm nearly sure it's the same handwriting."

Taking out his wallet from the inside pocket of his buckskin jacket, Raines opened it and took out the other notes he'd received. He opened them and with Dusty compared the writing.

"Looks the same to me," Dusty drawled and turned the newest paper over. He could see some vague marks on the paper and with his left hand took a bullet from the box on the table. Rubbing the lead tip of the bullet on the paper Dusty covered it with a black smudge. Not entirely covered though, for the depression made by a pencil writing on a sheet which lay over this one showed through. They were not distinct but for all that the words could be read: "T. Ortega. Lazy O, c/o Post Office, Backsight, Arizona Territory."

"Ortega again," growled Raines.

"That arrow wasn't fired by any Apache, not carrying the message," Dusty replied.

"And those bunch weren't tied in with any renegade white man," the Kid went on. "Which same only leaves us the one alternative."

"Where'd you learn big words like that, Lon?" asked Louise, coming up and having to say something to relieve the tension she felt.

"From a milk-faced lil blond dude gal I met on a wagon train," the Kid replied. "Gal about your si—"

"I was just about to ask Maisie if she could have her servants make up a meal for us," Louise interrupted mildly. "I seem to remember the last time I had trouble with you. Something about an apple pie."

The Kid grinned and raised his hands. "All right, gal, I quit."

"About this arrow?" asked Raines, not wishing to be sidetracked.

"Like Lon said, it couldn't be fired with the note on," Dusty answered. "So it must've been done after the attack. Everybody was excited and there was some coming and going. Anybody could've thrown it by Mrs. Simons' wagon."

Louise took the note, her face became hot and angry. "You mean Maisie could have thrown it!"

"Sure, then come back and pretended to throw a faint so's nobody would suspect her," agreed Dusty. "It could have been somebody trying to throw suspicion on Mrs. Simons, or just a coincidence the arrow landed where it did."

The girl opened her mouth to make an angry suggestion that they question Maisie, but before she could, she saw the train preacher coming. He told Raines he would be starting the burial ceremonies soon and asked if they could attend. Raines nodded but Dusty asked to be excused as he and his men had work to do.

"Do you reckon it was Mrs. Simons?" Mark asked after Louise and her father left to join the people around the graves.

"All I know is she can throw a gun nigh on as good as Cousin Betty."

Mark grunted for he knew how well Betty Hardin could handle a gun. Then he remembered Miss Considine and the time the Apaches broke through the circle.

"She's not alone in that," he drawled. "I saw Miss Considine shoot an Apache off Gantry's back in a shot that needed some close aiming, and not take long to do it. She handled a gun like she knew what it was about."

"What sort of gun?"

"Remington Beals from what I saw of it, Dusty," Mark replied. "Navy model."

"And Mrs. Simons used a long-barreled Navy Colt. They both handle a .36 bullet so we're no nearer to clearing either of them," Dusty drawled. "I'm going to have a talk with Mrs. Simons right now."

Maisie stood watching her two remaining helpers, one having been killed by an Apache bullet in the fight. The two men looked up as the Texans walked toward them and Maisie spoke in rapid Cantonese, apparently telling them they could go for, with half bows, the two Chinese men walked away.

"They'll attend to burying Wong. He's not a Christian and I reckon a man's entitled to be buried the way he wants," she said. "I should be with the folks at the buryings, but I'm not what you might call a real religious woman."

"It's your choice, ma'am," Dusty replied, noting the way the woman talked, the free and easy conversation. The woman was more than she appeared, more worldly than the widow she pretended to be. "Reckon we might feed with you?"

"Feel free. I told the boys to make enough for Louise and her folks."

"Like you to make up a couple of bundles of food for

the Kid and Red, too," Dusty went out. "I'm sending them out on a scout later today and want them to have food along."

"I'll see to it," Maisie replied.

"You over your faint, ma'am?"

"Sure, Captain. I must have been so scared I just let go and fell down in a swoon. It's funny, I never did anything like that before."

"Gets us all, ma'am," drawled the Kid sympathetically.

The burying was over and done with, and the Raines family returned to their wagons after a meal with Maisie. Dusty stood looking at the neatly wrapped and tied bundles of food on the table although he had so far not sent either of his friends out on a scout.

"Uh!" Louise muttered, looking at her grimy hands. "We haven't been able to take a bath since before Hammerlock, Dusty. Is there a place up ahead anywhere?"

"Not for two or three days," the Kid replied. "We're going to move fast in the morning to get clear of these Apaches in case they find a new old man chief."

"Why'n't you go around and tell the ladies to use the stream at the foot of the slope?" Dusty asked. "There's some bushes for cover further down and I'll stop any of the men following you. Then when you're through we can go down and tidy up."

The idea met with considerable approval, even among the people who lost loved ones in the fighting. Dusty watched the women streaming down the slope, saw both Miss Considine and Maisie among them and felt satisfied. The two Chinese were back with Maisie's wagon while Gantry and Miss Considine's remaining driver stood by the big woman's two Conestogas. There would be no chance of searching either.

That night as they sat alone at the Raines' fire Dusty asked Louise a question which considerably surprised her.

"What did you ladies wear down by the stream?"

Louise tried to appear shocked as she gasped, "Dusty!"

"Look, this's serious. What did you wear?"

"What does one usually wear at such a time?" Louise replied. "We went in—er—raw."

"All of you?"

"All I saw."

"How about Mrs. Simons and Miss Considine?"

"I didn't see either of them," Louise admitted. "They both went into the bushes away from us. I thought it was funny in Maisie's case as she'd always joined the rest of us when we bathed before—why do you ask?"

"Maybe I'm just curious."

"And maybe you aren't," she replied heatedly. "There's more to your asking than curiosity, Dusty, isn't there?"

"Yeah, I reckon there is. Back to Hammerlock, when Collins was killed, the Kid threw a bullet at whoever did it. Likely nicked him—or her."

Louise looked angrily at Dusty. "I'm tired of all these insinuations. Maisie has never given me any cause to suspect or dislike her."

"Sure, so there's no better person to be behind the trouble or working for whoever is behind it," drawled Dusty, holding his hand up in a peace sign. "Look at it this way, Louise, I'm not saying she's behind anything, only that things point to her being that way. If she was you reckon happen she'd sneak up behind you and beat you on your lil ole pumpkin every time she saw you, just to make sure you got good and suspicious about. I don't. She'd play it the way she is doing."

"Well I still trust her and I'm going right over there to—"

"You'll do nothing of the sort!" Dusty snapped, his voice taking on a warning note she knew so well. "I don't want her made suspicious, or guessing we're suspicious happen she's the one. Leave it lie. There'll not be anything more whoever it is can do before we reach Backsight."

The wagon train rolled on in the morning and the grief of their losses died slowly as every mile they rolled brought them nearer to Backsight. The Kid and Red made a wide sweep to come back with news that the Apaches had left their camp and headed south. Most likely they were making for some sacred ground to elect a new leader and make fresh medicine, guessed the Kid when he reported to Dusty.

So the final days and miles rolled behind them, each day seeing more penciled crosses on the Colonel's army maps. Each day the crosses drew closer to the great slash in the land known as the Grand Canyon and to the town of Backsight.

A new and light-hearted feeling filled the air. The train held a dance one night and a gay time was had by all. Miss Considine came out of her shell enough to prove she possessed a good soprano voice. The people went to bed tired and happy but Dusty never relaxed and it was hard on any sentry he found relaxing at his post on the night herd.

Several times in the days following the fight Louise tried to renew her discussion with Dusty or the others about Maisie's guilt or innocence. In this the girl found herself unsuccessful. The Texans evaded any conversation on that subject with the ease of matadors avoiding the charge of a bull.

Then one night just as the train was making its circle Louise sat by Dusty's side and watched. The Ysabel Kid rode up on his big white stallion; he came alone although he went out with Red Blaze in the morning.

"Where's Red?" Louise asked.

"Gone to see what Backsight looks like," replied the Kid, pointing across the range. "See that line of hills there, the one with the V nick at the top. There's a pass by it and about two miles on's the town. Likely the train'll be there soon after noon tomorrow and you'll have the wagons to Backsight by nightfall at the latest."

"I'll tell the folks," Louise began eagerly and started to turn her horse.

Dusty's hand shot out, catching her reins. "Hold it, hothead. We can't make it tonight and I don't want folks starting. There's no telling what we might run into and I want the folks to go in like a train, not in odd'ns."

"But Red rode on ahead," she protested.

"Sure, he knows the range and one man makes a damned

sight smaller target than a wagon. Besides, Mark and I'll be riding after him."

"Why?"

"Because I've known Cousin Red ever since we were old enough to throw spitballs at each other. He's plumb likely to get into a fight and wind up in jail."

The girl looked Dusty over and smiled. "Not when he's doing a job of work."

Dusty grinned. There were few people who could read Red Blaze's character the way the girl did.

"All right. Folks'll likely talk easier happen they don't know we're from the train," Dusty drawled. "Let's see the Colonel and then head on out."

The Kid groaned and protested that he'd done all the dirty work on the trip and was now being left behind when a good time stood ahead. The groaning was only a joke for he was pleased of a chance to rest his horse. Dusty gave him his orders, to keep his eyes and ears open for any sign of the travelers, any of them, leaving the train and heading for Backsight.

Red Blaze was riding into the town of Backsight just after dark. He timed his arrival with some care, coming in on the side away from the train. It was night and the arrival of a stranger was less likely to attract attention. There was less chance of his being recognized if, as they suspected, the tracks found at the mouth of the gap were caused by Collins' pard heading for Backsight. Red knew one wrong move might end with a bullet in his back. He also knew Dusty, Mark and the Kid would leave no stone unturned until they found his killer but the thought gave him little comfort.

The town of Backsight was little different to Red's eyes than a dozen or more such hamlets he'd seen throughout the West. There were not more than twenty houses at the outside, possibly half of them forming the main street. Two were saloons, one a run-to-seed store which would also serve as post office, although there were no telegraph wires to be seen. A building housed the land agent's office, which was dark and deserted, a padlock on the door. Further along was a small wooden structure which housed the county sheriff's office, jail and town marshal's office all in the space the cells took up in some of the larger towns. Red had seen many such hamlets; they rose when they were needed and hung on—only Backsight was going to grow instead of finally withering and fading away.

A man walked along the street ahead of Red and turned to look as the big claybank stallion came alongside him. The man halted, peering into the darkness as Red leaned forward and spoke to him.

"Howdy, friend," Red drawled. "Where'd a man leave his hoss, happen he wanted to leave it?"

"You want to leave one?"

"Nope. I'm only asking 'cause I'm curious."

The man grinned. "Curiosity's a terrible thing. They do say it killed the cat."

"I'm no cat, so chance telling me," Red answered, also grinning.

"Try behind the Alamo saloon down there. It's the civic pound but if anybody objects tell 'em you'll get drunk, go to jail and the hoss'll be there ready for the town marshal."

"Thanks. I like a helpful town," Red replied, turning the head of the claybank between the two houses indicated by the man.

The corral lay behind the houses and Red swung down from his horse. There was a pump close at hand, with a water trough fixed to it. Red watered and cared for the big stallion before removing the saddle. The corral was empty so he could leave his stallion without being worried about it fighting. He let the horse enter the corral and put the bar into place, then looked for somewhere he might leave his saddle until such time as he was able to find a place to sleep. He settled on a clump of bushes, carrying the heavy kak saddle to where it would be safe until he fetched it. He left the Spencer in the boot and laid the saddle carefully on its side, then turned as another rider came toward the corral.

The newcomer appeared to be a tall, slim young man

in cowhand-style clothes and with a splash of white showing across his body which puzzled Red at first. Then the young man halted his horse and dismounted. Red could now tell the white splash was formed of a sling on his right arm.

Moving forward in silence Red came toward the corral. He was about to speak when he saw two men walking between the houses, following the newcomer. They were a pair of Mexicans, even the darkness could not hide the shape of their sombrero hats or the silver filigree decoration on their coats and trousers.

"Hey, *gringo!*" one of the two said.

Red froze, standing by the side of the corral. The newcomer, a cowhand in his dress, turned to face the Mexicans, although he did not appear to be armed, or if he was did not have his gun in a holster at his side.

"Talking to me?"

"Who else?" came the reply from the shorter of the Mexicans. "Senor Fernandez is in town. He says for you or your sister to come over and see him. Most especially your sister."

"Tell him to go to hell!"

"He wouldn't like that, *gringo*. He wouldn't like it at all. More so from a man with only one arm. We don't like it either."

The two men moved nearer, fanning away from each other. Red stayed as he was, awaiting events and not wishing to take cards until he knew more about the game. Red might be a wild and reckless heller with a way of finding trouble and a habit of not wasting time before jumping into a fight. That only applied when he was on his own time. Doing a chore, even a self-appointed one like this, he was as cool and capable as any of the floating outfit.

"I've told Fernandez to stay well clear of my sister," the young cowhand replied, his stance more of a fist fighter than a good man with a gun. "And to keep his *bandidos* off my spread."

"*Bandidos*, Pablo!" purred the smaller man. "You hear what the *gringo* just call us and our friends."

"I heard and I didn't like it," replied the other, dropping his hand toward the butt of his gun. "I think we teach this *gringo* a lesson."

That gave Red warning he must cut in or see murder done. The Mexicans stood so far apart they had the cowhand whipsawed from the start but they were in line where Red could down both. His eyes took in the low hanging guns and the sheathed knives. These were not *vaqueros*, Mexican cowhands on a spree. They were a type he knew too well, a pair of bandits or he'd never seen their kind. In all the world, up to and including an Apache warrior after coups, there was no more cold-blooded a killer than a Mexican *bandido*. Either of that pair were willing to cut the cowhand down, one arm out of action or not.

"Saludos, senors!"

Red's soft spoken words were backed by the click of his right-hand Colt come to full cock. He knew Mexicans better than to speak without his gun in his hand, hammer back and ready to fall.

The Mexicans heard the click and read it for what it was. They also knew their position was as open to the man further along the corral as the cowhand stood open to them.

"You brought protection, *gringo*," the smaller man said in a disappointed tone. He was furthest from Red but knew he was clear of his *compadre* and open for a bullet.

"I never yet saw the gent afore," Red replied. "But there's surely going to be some introductions done if you don't get that damned hand well clear of your gun. Savvy?"

The small Mexican savvied. His hand fell from the revolver. The cowhand moved along the corral rail toward Red, the white butt of a revolver showing against his shirt as he walked, the butt pointing toward his left hand.

"Thanks, mister, I reckon their boss sent them to warn me against swearing out a warrant against him for cattle stealing."

"And I reckon they're just leaving," Red replied. "Which way do you want to leave, *hombres*. Walking or carried feet first?"

The two Mexicans exchanged glances and Red knew the answer without needing to be told. If they intended making a fight they would have done so without hesitation or looking to each other for guidance.

"There'll be other times," said the smaller man.

"There's always *manana*," agreed Red, neither relaxing nor holstering his Colt. "And comes morning the mission bells will greet the dawn—only you won't hear them if you're not away from here right *pronto*."

The two Mexicans turned on their heels and walked away. They were in plain view of Red all the time, and he watched them until they were out of sight before he holstered his gun. He knew better than trust any Mexican under those circumstances.

"Like to thank you, friend," the tall young cowhand remarked. "I near to knocked that one down when he said I should take Sister Sue to meet Fernandez."

Red suddenly realized he was further north than an area in which Mexican *bandidos* might be expected. No Texan who lived anywhere near the Rio Grande would make such a mistake.

"Happen you ever hit a greaser, kill him right straight after," Red warned. "If you don't he'll lay up and wait his chance to kill you. What was it all about?"

"Their boss moved down the canyon country below our place and we started to lose some stock. Then I caught one of his hands slapping a brand on a calf with a Lazy O mammy. Caught a bullet in the arm in the scuffle. I came into town to see if I can get any help from the law."

"Way you're talking it don't sound like you expect any," drawled Red.

"I don't. Biscuits Randle, him being our county deputy sheriff and town marshal rolled into one, well, he's a fine cook and brave enough. But he hasn't got the sort of brains or gun-skill that's needed to handle Fernandez. He's fast with a gun, real fast for a Mexican, is Fernandez and he's got some bad boys at his back."

"Here, let me help you with your saddle," Red suggested.

"Thanks, but I was only looking if there were any horses in the corral. I've a stable up at my place with a couple of empty stalls. Say, I don't think we've ever met. I'm Terry Ortega."

Not by a flicker of his face did Red allow the other man to know the name meant anything to him. He introduced himself and accepted the young rancher's suggestion that they take a couple of drinks at the Alamo. For all that, Red was puzzled. Terry Ortega was about his own age, a fairly good-looking and friendly young man. From his dress, Red noticed as they passed the lighted window of the saloon, Ortega was the owner of a middle-sized ranch. He did not look the sort of man with enough money or the necessary connections to hire professional killers all the way across country in Louisville.

"Where're you staying the night, Red?" asked Terry.

"With the sage-hens."

"Shucks, the sky's a poor roof. Come round to our town house for the night. It's not fancy but Sister Sue sees it gets kept tidy. It'll likely be a mite crowded being paynight and my crew on their way in. They'll be sleeping at the house."

None of which sounded like an arrogant and powerful rancher. Red accepted the invitation eagerly and they entered the Alamo saloon together. The saloon could not compare with the establishments of the big trail-end towns but served the needs of the local ranch crews. It sported sawdust on the floor, tables and chairs scattered around, a battered, bullet-pocked bar behind which stood a cheery-looking man who grinned broadly at Terry.

The atmosphere inside seemed friendly enough and Terry received boisterous greetings from the customers. Red took this chance to study the rancher in good light. His face was almost as freckled as Red's own, while his clothes, though of good quality were not new and showed signs of much washing and ironing. There did not appear to be anything out of the ordinary or in the least dangerous about him.

"Take two beers unless Terry's religious and don't touch the evil stuff," Red told the bartender. "Have something for yourself and then rustle me up a meal, will you."

"A meal," wailed the bartender. "Food he wants. Damned if I don't sell this place and head for some town that has an eating house."

"I don't know why somebody doesn't open an eating house here," Terry put in. "There's trade enough for it and we could use one. Could use a few things here even more, comes to that."

"This doesn't look a bad lil town," Red replied, as the bartender walked to a door behind the bar and bellowed an order for one son-of-a-bitch stew.

"Sure it's a nice lil town. But that's just what it is, little. Do you know Red, there's kids raising nine and ten years old here who haven't learned to read or write because we don't have a school. We've no doctor and if we want supplies or to send a telegraph message we have to trail to Hammerlock."

"More folks and a bigger town'd be the answer," Red drawled.

"It surely would," agreed Terry and no actor could have sounded more sincere than he did. "We heard rumors once or twice that folks were coming but they never arrived. I've tried to get the land agent to do something but he allows nobody wants to buy in on a place as far in the back country as this."

The words did not unduly surprise Red. Considine would not talk about Colonel Raines and his people in case he started a land rush with its following speculation on the resale. Backing his judgment of men, Red decided he would take Terry into his confidence and lay the cards down face up.

"Let's grab a seat before the boys come in," Terry suggested.

Before they could do so there was an interruption. The batwing doors burst open and half a dozen cowhands came in. They were a mixed bunch but they were real cowhands, not hired guns or hardcases. Two were near on old enough to be sitting around a stove and hard-wintering, two of middle age and the last two youngsters, fresh faced, brash, happy-go-lucky. One of the pair was blond haired, good-looking, and wore a violent red shirt with a multihued bandanna. Like the rest he carried an Army Colt at his side but there was none of the signs of the fast gun about any of the crew.

"She never saw me, I tells you!" the youngster whooped into the young man's ear.

"Wouldn't want to be you happen she did," replied the other. "Terry, Duke here done wide-looped Sue's fresh baked apple pie."

"Then may the Lord have mercy on his soul, 'cause Sister Sue won't have any on his fool hide when she finds out."

"She won't find out. I'm too slick," Duke answered modestly.

The cowhands crowded around the table to which their boss and Red moved. Red studied them, for a man could learn much by the kind of hands a ranch hired. All Red learned stood to Terry's favor for the cowhands were the sort any decent ranch owner would be proud and satisfied to hire. The good natured chaff which flew back and forward showed they were all friends of long standing.

"You boys better get acquainted with Red Blaze from Texas," Terry told his crew. "He pulled two of Fernandez's men off my back in the corral."

The cowhands greeted Red warmly, their gratitude for his actions at the corral there but unsaid. The other youngster, Tommy Malveny, demanded to be told the full story. The crew showed their appreciation of Red's actions but one of the old timers, the withered cowhand called Tombstone, eyed Red up and down.

"Now you done got Fernandez after you."

"Hush your fool ole mouth," whooped Duke. "You'll be a-scaring Red off real soon if you don't."

"He don't talk nor smell that bad—yet," drawled Red.

There would be no chance of talking quietly to Terry, Red saw. He was invited into a poker game, with the express intention of being shown how the game got played in Arizona Territory. Red's luck at poker was talked of wherever it had been seen. That same luck stood high as the cards dropped on the rough table top in the Alamo, by which token the Lazy O crew found themselves sadder and wiser men when the game broke up and they rose to head for the bar.

Red scooped his winnings from the table. The financial gain was not high for they played a five- to ten-cent limit. However, the game served a purpose in allowing Red to get to know the others better. The more he saw, the more certain Red became that Terry Ortega was entirely innocent of any threat to the train.

"My arm's beginning to throb a mite," Terry remarked as they stood at the bar and Red spent his winnings treating his opponents. "I'm going to bed."

"I'll come with you," Red replied, seeing a chance of making private talk.

"The night's still young and so are we," whooped Duke. "We'll stay on and enjoy it while we can."

"Don't wake up Sister Sue," Terry warned. "She'll raise lumps on your fool heads if you do."

"Who's this Sister Sue?" Red inquired.

"My kid sister," Terry answered in noncommittal tone.

"She sure is," agreed Duke. "Anyways she's staying with the Leylands tonight so we're safe enough."

Red and Terry collected their horses and gear, then walked toward the small white-painted house at back of town. Terry opened the gate in the picket fence and a shot sounded from the main street somewhere. Neither took much notice for shots were no uncommon sound. It would most likely only be some cowhand letting off steam. A second shot crashed out from the same direction as Terry unlocked the house door. Then they heard the sound of rapidly departing hooves.

"Every paynight's the same," chuckled Terry. "I bet that's ole Biscuits chasing them out of town."

The house, a small, two-story, frame building, neatly

if not expensively furnished, showed signs of care that a
woman would lavish on her home. Red stabled and cared
for the horses then carried both saddles inside, laying them
carefully on their sides in a corner. No cowhand ever set
his saddle down on its shirts or left it where clumsy feet
might tread on and damage it.

While Red cared for the horses, Terry brewed coffee and
by the time Red entered the dining-room had it on the table.
While they drank the coffee, Red took his chance to have
a serious talk with the young rancher.

"You got any enemies, Terry?" he asked.

"None that I know of, 'cepting Fernandez. Why?"

Quickly Red told about the coming wagon train. He saw
the pleasure on the other man's face die as he went on about
the threats and the notes which bore Terry's address in-
dented on the back.

"I can't think who'd do it," Terry stated firmly. "Or why
they'd try to blame me. I want a town here, so did my
father before me. I've been trying to get Considine, he's
the land agent, to do something about it."

Not having mentioned Miss Considine's presence with
the train or the fact that she gave an entirely different picture
of Terry, Red was curious to learn more about the land
agent.

"What's this Considine like?"

"Big, good looking, smart. He's efficient and I'm surprised he stays in a place like this when he could be somewhere bigger and offering him a better chance."

They talked on for a time but reached no conclusion as
to who might want to make trouble for Terry. Red glanced
across the room at a tintype photograph of a snub-nosed
and very pretty girl of about twelve years old which rested
on the sideboard by the wall.

"That your kid sister?" he asked.

"Sure, sweet-looking lil thing, isn't she?"

"Why sure," agreed Red, thinking she looked as if butter
wouldn't melt in her mouth.

"You can use her room, Red boy, it'll be quieter than

down here. She won't need it as she's staying with the Leylands tonight. Major Leyland runs a spread out beyond our north line. Real nice gent, rode in the 8th Minnesota Volunteers in the War."

"Sounds like a real mean cuss to me," grinned Red.

"You Johnny Rebs are all the same. If he wore the blue he's got horns and a forked tail," chuckled Terry. "Anyway, Major Leyland's like me, he's been at the governor to get folks to build up out here. I'm going to bed. Comes morning I'll introduce you to Sister Sue."

Red did not show any great enthusiasm at the offer. He liked to meet good-looking blond girls but much preferred their ages to be in the region of his own age, and there were limits to how much younger he would accept on a friendly basis. Twelve years old, that was well below Red's limit for social acquaintance.

Terry grinned as he watched Red walking ahead of him up the stairs to the bedrooms. Red Blaze looked like getting a tolerable surprise when he met up with Terry's little sister.

CHAPTER NINE

Miss Raines Meets Miss Ortega

DUSTY FOG and Mark Counter rode into the town of Back-sight at about the time the poker game was coming to an end at the Alamo. They'd taken their time, come by the short route and so the horses were still fresh when they drew rein before the Arizona State saloon.

"That's looking forward a tidy mite," drawled Dusty, indicating the saloon's name board.

"Must be wanting to save having it repainted when they get to be a state," Mark replied. "Let's look inside."

They left the horses standing at the hitching rail and stepped inside the saloon. The Arizona State was no larger nor was it better furnished than the other establishment along the street. There were some two dozen or more men in the bar but none gave the newcomers more than a scant glance before returning to whatever they were doing.

The bartender leaned on the bar, polishing glasses with a cloth which had seen better days. He was a tall, lean and mournful man, his face more suited to an undertaker than to the owner of a fairly prosperous saloon. At the other side of the bar, leaning his elbows on it and with a beer schooner almost hidden in his hand was a huge, powerful-looking man. He stood almost as tall as Mark and was a fair bit heavier. His shirt sleeves were rolled up to expose powerful arms, his Levi's were new and his shoes flat heeled, something no cowhand would wear. On his vest was the badge of town marshal but he did not wear a gun. His sleepy eyes were on the two Texans, taking in the way their guns hung, then every detail of their dress.

"Two beers, colonel," drawled Mark as they came to the bar.

Eddy Last, the owner of the saloon, extracted two bottles of beer and poured them with bored skill. "You're new hereabouts, aren't you?" he asked.

The question was well within the bounds of Western polite conversation. A bartender, along with a barber and a livery barn owner being a member of the privileged class who could ask such a question of a stranger without giving offense.

"Aren't old any place," Mark replied.

"Would you be looking for work?"

"Never took none to it, friend," Dusty answered.

Last glanced down at their dress, noting their hard and work-toughened hands. They were the hands of a working cowhand but they also bore the marks of a man who regularly handled his guns. Yet neither Texan showed the signs of being professional gunhands. Both were tophands with cattle. Hired killers who sold their guns to the highest bidder, they most certainly were not.

"Lazy O could use a couple of good hands," Last went on.

"Lazy O," drawled Dusty. "That'd be the Ortega place, wouldn't it?"

"Sure. Terry's a good boss. He could use some extra hands happen he aims to clear that range south of his place."

"We're just passing through, colonel," Mark answered. "Can we get a meal in here?"

"Sure, I've a cook back there."

Dusty and Mark took their beer and food to a table, eating and drinking as they watched the coming and going. From the various groups they guessed the ranch crews were in town with their pay. Watching the men Dusty could see no sign of trouble between the crews. With his knowledge of the range and the men who worked it, Dusty could read the signs and would have seen signs of friction between the men if any showed.

"Wonder where Cousin Red is," said Dusty, pushing his empty plate away.

"He'll be around unless he's found some trouble," Mark replied. "Which same's more than likely. Let's have another beer then head back to the train."

"I'll get them, see if I can learn anything from the barkeep."

Last moved along the bar toward Dusty, then he stopped, his eyes went to the doors of the saloon. Dusty glanced into the bar mirror but did not turn at the sight of the five Mexicans by the door. He knew their type without needing to be told. *Bandidos* every one of them. The man who stood ahead of the others caught the eye. Tall, slim, with a graceful, lithe poise which told of skill with a blade, be it saber, rapier or plain fighting knife. Yet no knife showed. Only the ornate cast metal-stocked Navy Colt in the gunfighter's holster, which appeared to be his sole armament. He was a well-dressed, arrogant young man whose face bore the hint of real cruelty of all his kind.

Talk in the saloon died away to nothing and the ticking of the wall clock sounded loud. Eddy Last caught Dusty's unasked question, and with barely a lip movement to show he spoke, muttered:

"It's Fernandez. He's bad medicine."

Dusty turned slowly so he could look the bad medicine over. He was not impressed for in some circles Dusty was said to be real bad medicine himself. A Texan born and raised, Dusty had been trained in a school which claimed one white man to be the equal of two Mexicans—four if

the white man be born in the Lone Star State and over ten
years old.

Crossing the room, Fernandez halted before the big
sleepy-eyed lawman, but not within reaching distance of
him. There was a movement from the bar leaving the burly
man clear but Dusty stayed where he was, within arm's
length of the town marshal. Fernandez flicked just the one
look at Dusty, then ignored him as a factor. Lifting his hand
so the fingers spread over the butt of the holstered Colt, he
smiled and looked more evil than the devil himself.

"*Saludos, señor* lawman," he purred.

The big man stayed leaning against the bar, his sleepy
eyes went to the hand, measuring the distance between
himself and the Mexican.

"What're you wanting, Fernandez?" he asked.

"A word to the wise, that's all. Soon will come a man
with many lies about me. If you value your life don't listen
to him."

"What sort of lies?"

"That my men are stealing his cattle."

"And are they?"

A hard glow came to the Mexican's eyes, his face lost
the smile. "I gave you a gentle hint. Now I tell you. Keep
clear of me. The badge is like a target to me and when I
see one I always feel I should shoot at it."

The big man's muscles bunched, his figure tensed and
the mocking sneer came to the Mexican's face. His four
men also tensed, their hands hooking into belts and close
to their guns.

Dusty took all this in. He knew the Mexican was fast,
very fast. The burly town marshal might try and jump Fernandez but would be dead before he could get his big hands
closed on the Mexican. To deal with such a man there was
only one answer. To be faster with your own gun.

Fernandez stood with a mocking sneer still playing on
his lips. Then he saw the small cowhand move, hand going
out to remove the badge from Biscuits Randle's vest and

pin it on his own shirt. Then his hands went to his side and he faced the Mexican, cold challenge in his eyes.

"So a badge is like a target," Dusty said quietly. "Use it!"

The big man half-turned, an angry look on his face. He was no coward and kept the law in Backsight without the aid of a gun, dealing fairly but firmly with the cowhands. Then the anger died and Randle stood still for he was no man's fool. In his time out West, Biscuits Randle could claim to have seen some of the fastest men in action. Here stood one who was the peer if not better than any he ever saw.

"Have you hired a man to do your fighting, Randle?" Fernandez asked, wondering if this was the man who stood by Terry Ortega earlier.

"He hired nobody and you well know it," replied Dusty. "Take off your gun belt so you're on his ground and see if I'm right."

"Happen they all takes off their belts I'll take 'em tooth 'n' claw, friend, see if I don't," Randle put in. "All five at once."

"The son of a *grandee* does not brawl like a common peasant," snorted Fernandez.

"Then," Dusty drawled mildly, "That only leaves you and me."

"As you say, *señor*. Just you and I."

The crowd fell silent after a brief mumble of surprised comment when they saw Dusty cut in. They all knew there could only be one outcome of all this. Hands would flash to guns, powder would burn and at least one man die, for Fernandez would never back down before the small Texan. Suddenly Dusty appeared small no longer. Suddenly he appeared to be the tallest man in the room.

Fernandez smiled a cold, deadly smile which did not reach his eyes. His men were at his back, full ready to back him if it was needed. With that thought in his mind Fernandez dropped his hand toward the fancy butt of the Army Colt.

Half a second from the start of his move he was dead.

Dusty's right hand crossed, bringing the Colt from his
left side, the hammer drawn back under his thumb as it slid
clear of leather, all set to fire when, half a second later, it
was lined. The shot sounded loud in the room. Powder
smoke whirled. Fernandez jerked backward, his gun clear
of leather, but it pointed down and his lifeless hand allowed
it to fall to the floor. Then he went down after it.

The thing was over and done with so fast that Fernandez'
men were given no chance to make a move. They stood as
if frozen as Fernandez crashed to the ground among them.

Smoke still dribbled up from the muzzle of Dusty's Colt
as he lined on the four remaining Mexicans. It only needed
one of them to make a move and bring the others into the
fight. That one was not forthcoming. Until an instant before
they stood behind a leader who called every play for them.
Now he lay dead and not one of them could supply the
personality to bring the others into cohesive action.

"Which way does it go?" Dusty asked, giving them no
chance to band together under one leader.

"Fernandez wasn't our friend, *señor*," replied one of the
men.

"We didn't like him one little bit," a second agreed.

"Take him with you!"

Dusty gave the order as the men turned. Three of them
bent and lifted the body from the floor then headed for the
door with it. The fourth followed, his hand sliding to the
butt of his knife as he went. The Colt pinwheeled on Dusty's
finger then slid back into leather, he turned back to the bar
and asked the rather pale-looking Eddy Last to get two more
beers.

The men carrying Fernandez passed through the bat-
wings. The fourth man came around with his knife gripped
ready. His arm swung back and the blade of the knife
flickered in the bar lamps.

Mark Counter did not even rise. His big right hand
fetched out its Colt and flame lashed from the long barrel.
The .44 bullet struck the Mexican just as his arm started

its descent, spinning the man through the batwing doors. The knife went into the floor, sinking in deep.

"Thanks, Mark," drawled Dusty over his shoulder as he picked up the glasses.

"Any ole time at all, Dusty," Mark replied.

Talk welled up in the saloon again. They heard rapidly departing feet and a man went to the doors, coming back with word that two bodies lay on the sidewalk while the other Mexicans were afork their horses and heading out of town like the devil after a yearling.

Randle followed Dusty to the table, trying to decide who the small Texan might be. He was one of the good guns, one of the top guns, that magic-handed group who could draw, shoot and make their hit in much less than a second.

"Say, sorry, friend," drawled Dusty, setting down the glasses and removing the badge. "Here's your badge. You couldn't have got to him without taking his lead in your teeth, which same's plumb bad for the digestion."

"Thanks," replied Randle, pinning his badge on once more. "Happen I could throw a gun as fast as you I'd take to wearing one."

"Them drinks are on the house, gents," Last said as he came up carrying a tray with whisky glasses and a bottle of his best on it. "You'd better take one Biscuits. I thought you'd jump Fernandez with your bare hands and I didn't reckon you'd get very far with it."

"Say, I'm Biscuits Randle, whatever law there is in this section, and this's Eddy Last."

"Howdy. I'm Dusty Fog and this here's Mark Counter."

Talk welled up around the room at the two names. The cowhands, and most of the crowd were cowhands, recalled they'd heard about Mark Counter and the big Texan looked all of the hearing. However, it took some believing that the small man could really be Dusty Fog. Then they recalled the way Fernandez came to die and knew he told the truth.

"They left Fernandez and the other, took a greaser stand-off," the man at the door announced.

"I'll tend to them," Randle remarked and slouched away from the table. He called to men to help him. From the response it was plain the cowhands of the town liked and respected him.

Several more men gathered around the table. They had the appearance of ranchers and all were eager to meet the Hondo gun wizard and not a little curious at what brought the segundo of the mighty OD Connected ranch from Texas to their small town.

"That Fernandez and his bunch have been running this country ragged for a fair piece now," Last remarked after introducing the ranchers. "Ole Biscuits's brave enough but he's no hand with a gun, 'cepting maybe a ten gauge. Still he'd've made a try at fetching Fernandez in if he had to then there'd be killing. Biscuits and more might've gone under for we wouldn't have stood by and watched him killed. I reckon we owe you a vote of thnaks, Cap'n Fog."

Dusty laughed and waved a deprecatory hand. He had hoped to meet Terry Ortega and form an opinion of the man but the owner of the Lazy O was not present. For all that Dusty doubted if a man as smart as the one behind the threats to the train would commit the stupid mistake of allowing his name and address to be found twice.

"Are you staying hereabouts, Captain Fog?" asked Major Leyland, a rather stiff and military looking rancher.

"Nope, just drifting through. This's a nice little town though. Could do with being a mite larger for all of that."

"It sure could," Leyland agreed. "I can't see why the land office doesn't wake itself up. We've thought of taking a petition to the governor and see what he can do for us."

"Passed a fair-sized wagon train headed this way. Coming here, the folks do tell," Mark drawled, catching his cue from Dusty.

"Nesters?" growled the man next to Leyland.

"Nope!" Dusty brought the answer in to clear up that problem. He knew how the open range rancher felt about nesters, the small farmers and the trouble they brought in their wake.

"Like I said," Mark went on. "They're coming here to build a town."

"What'll the Ortegas say to that?" asked Last, not knowing he was asking the one question Dusty wanted to hear.

"If I know young Terry and Sue they'll likely throw up the first house with their bare hands," laughed Leyland. "They've both been bending my ear every time they saw me, ever since their pappy died and he was as bad before them."

"They want a town here bad?" asked Dusty.

"More than any of us. Their mother died giving birth to a baby; it died too. Wasn't a doctor within a hundred miles or more. Ever since that the Ortega famly haven't given any of us any peace about having a proper town here so we'd have all we wanted and be independent of Hammerlock."

Dusty watched Leyland and saw the rancher to be serious. Talk welled up in the room and the ranchers escorted Dusty and Mark to the bar so that they could answer questions about what the wagon train contained. It was clear that the new citizens of Backsight would meet with approval among the old inhabitants.

"Some purty and unmarried gals!" whooped a cowhand to the man who stood next to him, a rider who sported a bushy beard. "I told you you'd regret growing that lot."

It was at that moment Eddy Last decided to take control of the situation as became a leading member of the community. He pounded lustily on the bar top and raised a yell which might be expected to raise echoes the entire length of the Grand Canyon.

"Order. Hey! Give me order!"

"I'll take another couple of beers," Mark replied.

Last waited until the laughter and talk died down, then leaned forward and bellowed, "Boys, I hereby proposes, seconds and thirds that we all goes out there and meets these folks tomorrow. Show them that they're real welcome in Backsight."

The yell of agreement almost jolted the bottles from behind the bar.

"Yowee!" whooped Mark, winking at the big burly rancher by his side. "Ain't he the living genius. Deserves to be showed respect!"

With that, two huge hands shot across the bar. Last saw them an instant too late, for they closed on his vest and he was lifted over the bar like he weighed no more than a baby. The whooping and yelling cowhands passed Last from hand to hand over their heads, right around the room, back to Mark and the rancher, who lowered him gently but head first back over the bar. He came up red of face, throwing curses at Texas in general and a certain overgrowed blond schoolkid in particular, but for all that his hands were busy serving drinks to celebrate the coming of the wagon train.

Louise Raines was unable to sleep. She rolled and tossed on her bed but the thought of her new home being so close prevented sleep from coming. The first red streak of dawn was in the sky as she rolled out of her blankets and dressed. Then climbing out of the wagon she took up her saddle and went to where the horse was tethered.

"Where'd you reckon you're going, gal?"

Louise jumped slightly at the words and turned to find the Ysabel Kid behind her. The saddle was half on her horse and she replied, "I felt like taking a ride. Exercise my horse."

"Why sure. Keep your eye on that V notch, then when you get to it you'll see the town. Tell Dusty nobody left the train last night."

The girl turned and stared at him. "How did you know?"

"I told you, you'd never make a poker player. Get going. I don't reckon your pappy'd approve."

Louise made good time as she crossed the range, she found the pass through the hills and soon after rode along the deserted main street of Backsight, seeing for the first time the town which was to be her home. The whinny of a horse led her to the corral behind the buildings. There was a fair bunch of horses in the corral and to one side Dusty's paint grazed alongside Mark's bloodbay. There was no sign of Red's claybank and this worried Louise. She did not know of Red's meeting with Terry Ortega and wondered where he might be.

The party in celebration of the wagon train's arrival had gone on until the small hours of the morning and most of the festive cowhands were still fast asleep in the brush or wherever they spent the night. The town lay silent, deserted and Louise had seen nobody since she rode in.

Swinging down from the horse Louise prepared to remove the saddle and leave it in the corral with the others. She heard the sound of another horse behind her, then a feminine voice said:

"Now that's what I call a real fine hoss."

Louise turned to look at the speaker. She was a small, shapely and very pretty young woman with curly, fairly short blond hair. A Stetson was thrust back on her head, her face while tanned was snub-nosed and bore a friendly smile which added to the merry sparkle in her blue eyes. Her clothes were a tartan shirtwaist thrust into old, washed-out blue jeans which hung cowhand style outside high-heeled and fancy-stitched boots. She stood about an inch smaller than Louise but her figure was rich and full with hard firm muscles under the skin.

"He's all right," Louise replied, liking the look of the other girl.

"Bluegrass country thoroughbred," remarked the small girl. "Don't see a sight of them this side of the Big Muddy."

"I brought him from Kentucky," Louise replied, looking at the mean, vicious little cowpony which the girl secured to the corral well clear of her own horse. Its ears were flattened down and it tried to kick sideways while swinging its head to snap at the girl who avoided the bite with ease. "You've picked a bad one there."

The girl laughed. Louise liked her even more when she laughed for there was the world of delight in the laugh. She hoped the other girl would be a neighbor.

"Ole Tonto's a sawed-off lump of perversity," the girl answered merrily. "I sure don't know why I keep him in my string. The boys at the spread allow it's because he's the only thing with a meaner temper than mine. Say, I haven't seen you around town. My name's Sue Ortega."

CHAPTER TEN

Miss Raines Indulges in Fisticuffs

LOUISE lost her friendly smile at the words. "Are you related to Terry Ortega?"

"You might say that," Sue replied. "He's my big brother."

Louise was much like her father in hot temper. She spoke without a thought of the result of her words.

"Why has he tried to stop us getting here?" she gasped hotly. "What does he mean by trying to have my father killed?"

"Say, easy gal, easy," drawled Sue, not losing her temper, suspecting the other girl to be a victim of cowhand humor. "It's not often he goes after fathers. Mostly it's the other way around, they come after him with a scattergun and a marrying gleam in their eyes."

If Sue had treated the matter more seriously it might have been explained away. Unfortunately she did not and Louise suspected something more than friendly good nature behind the words. She thought Sue recognized her and was playing with her like a cat with a mouse.

"You know what I mean!" she snapped. "Your brother

hired men to try and kill my father in Nashville, then again on the trail. Then you sent the Apaches after our wagon train."

The laughter left Sue's eyes and her voice dropped hard and cold. It was a warning sign which any of the Lazy O crew and most of Backsight's citizens could read. When Sue Ortega stopped smiling, it became time to hunt for cover.

"Just what in all hell are you yapping about?" Sue demanded.

"You know!" Louise answered, her voice rising a shade. "You know full well what your brother has been—"

"Now wait a minute," Sue put in, taking Louise's appearance in for what it was. "Did a good-looking young cowhand with a bright red shirt and a bandanna you could see from here to the Texas line tell you about Terry?"

"You know it wasn't. Your brother doesn't want us to build a town here."

"A town! Now I know you're fooling me. Terry and I want a town here. We've been hoping one would be built but it never has."

Louise stared at the other girl. "You're a liar!"

Which proved to be about the worst thing Louise could have said. Sue, range born and bred, lived in a world where the word "liar" was never used unless followed by the crash of shots or the thud of a blow. She moved, her hand coming around in a smooth swing, the fist catching Louise on the cheek and spinning her into the corral rail. The ranch girl was quivering with fury but just managed to hold herself in check.

"A joke's a joke, but this has gone far enough!"

Louise came away from the rail with a squeal of rage. Never since childhood had another woman struck her and her rage burst like the flood waters of a dam. She hurled forward with fists swinging wildly, feeling them strike the other girl, then she was sent staggering by another hard punch.

"All right!" Sue hissed. "If that's how you wa—"

The words ended as Louise swung her own fist. In her childhood around the Army camps, Louise had learned to look after herself in the hair-yanking brawls. Jim Lourde taught her to use her fists and although she gave up such habits as she grew up, the instinct was still there.

The girls hurled themselves at each other once more. They seemed to come together in midair, hands swinging, then digging into hair. Each girl tore and pulled at the other's hair with one hand, swinging, gripping and punching with the other. They spun around a few times then went to the ground, rolling over with wild thrashing arms and legs. It was a female brawl with no skill in it as they rolled over and over to the accompaniment of squeals, screams and yells of pain and fury.

Louise rolled the other girl away and started to come to her feet but Sue tackled her around the waist in a dive which brought them both crashing down again. Louise wrapped her legs around Sue and squeezed hard, her muscles, toughened by the long journey, brought a gasp of pain. Desperately and by blind instinct Louise tried to hold the grip and Sue tried just as hard to get out of it. Gripping one of the constricting legs Sue forced it up, ducked under it and caught a punch which sent her rolling over. Louise was at her straight away and they sailed over to fight their way to their feet again.

"Had enough?" Sue gasped, fists clenched, hair tangled and breasts heaving.

Louise brought across a punch which staggered Sue and came in. The girls used their fists like two men for a time, swinging wild punches with connected or missed, depending on luck. Then they closed with each other again and went sprawling to the ground. In their thrashing wild tangle, they did not notice the way they rolled, straight toward the wildly stamping hooves of the paint cowpony.

Red Blaze and Terry Ortega came walking toward the Lone Star saloon when they heard the sounds of the fight behind the houses. Terry looked at Red with a grin and said:

"Sounds like my lil sister's in town. Let's go and meet her."

The two men found the bout of female fisticuffs going at full pace. Louise knelt on the ground at a temporary disadvantage for Sue was behind her, swinging wild slaps and blows at the other girl. Louise grabbed over her shoulder and caught Sue's hair and heaved, bringing the ranch girl over then piling on to her again.

"Stop 'em, Red!" Terry yelled, for they rolled toward the stamping pinto.

Red jumped forward. He recognized Louise and wondered what brought her to town, then tangled her in this unladylike, wildcat brawl. He was also interested in the other girl. Happen Terry called it right and this was his sister, the picture at the house must be old, her being full growed and right nice looking. That showed even all mussed-up and hawk-wild like she appeared right now.

There was no time for thought, or southern chivalry, for the girls had rolled near the horse. Red bent, grabbing one of each girl's thrashing feet, hauling them bodily clear and not a moment too soon. The pinto's lashing, stamping hooves drove down to where Louise's head lay a moment before.

The problem of stopping the fight did not cease, for the girls clung to each other, swinging wild slaps and punches. Red bent, grabbing Sue who happened to be on top at that moment then hauled her clear of Louise. The girls tried to cling on and land more blows but Red tore them apart. Sue screamed wildly as she struggled to get free and defend herself from Louise who was getting to her feet, eyes wild with rage and fists clenched ready to attack again.

Terry jumped forward, his good arm going around Louise's waist to hold her. Luckily for him Louise felt exhausted and suddenly realized what she'd been doing. She gave a gasp and went limp in Terry's grip, every inch of her body aching and burning with shame at her actions. She began to sob and hung in Terry's grip.

Sue did not sob. She struggled wildly and one of her

thrashing feet caught Red on the shin, causing him to use some words he did not often employ in the presence of the opposite sex.

"Lemme loose!" Sue screamed wildly. "Lemme at her, you long-eared, spavined no-account drink of dirty water!"

Which proved to be an unfortunate choice of terms.

"Water, ma'am," drawled Red, scooping the girl under his arm so she could not use her arms and her legs thrashed harmlessly. "Why, sure, anything to oblige a lady."

With that Red carried the girl to the water trough and held her over it.

"Lemme go, da—!" Sue growled, still struggling. Then for the first time became aware of her position in relation to the water trough. "No! Don't you d—"

The words ended in a gurgling yell and splash as Sue landed face down in the water, going right under and coming up again with unladylike curses spluttering like firecrackers from her lips. Red extended a hand, placed it on Sue's head and pushed her back under water. On rising again Sue was silent, she twisted her head to look up, grinned and said:

"Let up, red-top. I'm good now."

Reaching down Red helped the girl from the water. Ignoring the wet state of her clothes, Sue turned to look at her brother as he comforted Louise by the corral. Sue reached up and gently touched her swollen right eye, winced, removed the hand then gave a gasp and pulled her shirt-waist together finding enough buttons remaining to allow her to retain some semblance of respectability.

"All right, Sue," Terry growled, bringing Louise forward to sit her on the edge of the trough. "What started all this?"

"That's what I'd like to know," Sue replied, holding her jaw and working it before carrying on. "Said something about my hoss and we got on all right until I mentioned my name. Then she started on about you setting Apaches to kill her pappy. I thought Duke'd met her and been jobbing her at first. Reckon we lost our tempers and landed on each other tooth 'n' claw, which same this gal's not bad at."

Louise had in some measure regained control of herself.

She managed to maker her blouse meet and regain modesty, then recognized Red for the first time.

"Red," she gasped, indicating Sue. "This's Terry Ortega's sister."

"Do tell," drawled Red and nodded to Sue. "Right pleased to meet you, ma'am. And seeing's how we're getting acquainted, Miss Louise Raines, this here's Terry Ortega's sister's only brother."

It took Louise a long moment to understand Red's meaning. She was gently feeling her left eye with a careful fingertip but jerked it away and stared at a solemn Terry then at Red and Sue, who grinned at her surprise.

"Then you're—"

"That's right, Miss Louise. I'm Terry Ortega."

Sue sat up and rubbed her hip where it hurt from either hitting the ground or a kick, she was not sure which. She turned a warm grin toward Red. "I'm sorry I called you all those names, even if they were true and I meant them. Say, Louise gal, what started you into hair-yanking with me? Not that it wasn't as good a round as I ever had."

Louise stared at the Ortega family and made a decision. They were such nice and friendly people even though she and Sue had fought, that she felt she could trust them. Sue listened to Louise's explanation without a word then at the end let out a couple of salty curses which drew an admiring grin from Red. Louise ended her explanation and after Sue's comments went on:

"I'm really sorry, Sue. I can't think what came over me."

"I did for one thing," Sue grinned. "Say, I bet we have two dandy black eyes comes night. Won't that start the gals around town talking?"

Louise took Sue's hand, feeling the other girl's firm and strong grip. In her childhood Louise had been involved in more than one hair-yanking brawl, for she led a tomboyish existence around the boot camps of the Army. Since growing up she put aside such things as beneath the dignity of a lady. In a flash she saw Sue did not regard the affair in such a light and any attempt to show disapproval would end their friendship, for the ranch girl was willing to become a friend.

"Say," drawled Red. "Nobody's introduced me. Miss Ortega, I'm Red Blaze of the Rio Hondo country of Texas."

"No," scoffed Sue, "I'd never have guessed, Montana maybe, even New York, but I'd never have guessed you came from Texas."

"Happen I'd known there was a gal like you in Arizona I'd've been out this way afore now."

Sue studied Red for a long moment, ignoring the water which still dripped from her hair and soaked clothing. "That sounds like it's been said more'n once. How many gals have you tried it on?"

"A couple here, a couple there, you know how it is," Red replied.

"Can't say I do, being a gal myself."

"Never meant it afore though," drawled Red.

Something of a blush came to Sue's cheeks and to hide her confusion she turned toward Louise and said, "It's all right for you. I got tossed in the hoss trough."

Louise read the challenge and did not hesitate for a moment. Being in a new land she knew a new standard of values lay on things. Sue's dare lay cast before her like a thrown-down gauntlet and Louise knew she must take it up. Without a word she flopped back into the water, going right under, then emerged with a cool and dignified look on her face.

"There now," she said. "Satisfied?"

The challenge had been taken up, met and topped by Louise's cool and calm action. Sue threw back her head, laughter pealing out, delight glowing in her eyes. Red watched the girl and knew she and no other meant everything in the world to him. His own laugh rang in then and Louise started. Terry watched them for a moment, then he too was laughing.

"Let's go down to our place, Louise," Sue gasped at the end, wiping tears from her eyes. "Wowee! Laughing's sure hard on the face. You pack a mean right hand, gal. I'll be eating mush for a week. I've got some dry clothes that should ought to fit us both."

The girls walked away side by side and the two young men followed. Red managed to tear his eyes from Sue for long enough to ask a question which had puzzled him ever since he met the distaff side of the Ortega family.

"How come you talk northern and Sue sounds like she was born in Dixie?"

"Reckon I got it from mother and she caught her accent from dad," Terry replied. "I reckon at times Sue should have been a boy."

"Which same's one thing we don't agree on."

Terry looked at Red for a moment and a grin came to his face. "The first thing I know you'll be sparking my lil sister."

"Likely. My pappy always told me never to go sparking a gal unless you know she can cook."

"Well, she can and real good."

By this Red got the idea his sparking would not be unwelcome. They made for the Ortega house where the girls went upstairs to change into dry clothes. From the sounds of giggling and chatter which accompanied the changing, Miss Raines and Miss Ortega held no grudge about their recent fight.

Red sat down, his face was more serious as he looked Terry over. "We'd best see cousin Dusty and let him make what he can out of the tries at killing Colonel Raines and blaming you for it."

"Cousin Dusty?"

"Sure, he's with the train. I never mentioned it," Red drawled and seeing Terry still did not understand went on, "Dusty Fog."

"Is *he* your cousin?" asked Terry.

"Has been ever since I was a button."

Red was still talking about his illustrious cousin when the girls came downstairs. They wore dry clothes, Louise felt just a trifle self-conscious in a pair of Sue's jeans and

Terry's admiring glance brought a blush to her cheeks which did not go with her puffy and discolored left eye. Both she and Sue were well on the way to showing a beautiful black eye. It was the only visible sign of their fight, although both carried bruises on their bodies.

"Let's go along to Uncle Eddy's place," Sue suggested. "The boys'll likely be there and I want to raise lumps on the head of a certain pie-stealing heller. Sure I know Duke took it and he'll likely be at breakfast now. Anyways it'll save us ladies cooking."

"Never saw a couple of ladies acting like you pair down at the corral," Red put in. "Nor sporting eyes like those, neither."

Sue's reply came in a pungent and hide-searing blast of rangeland profanity which somehow sounded natural and not in the least disgusting from her lips. She offered Red her arm in a parody of the polite manner her mother tried to teach her.

"You may escort me to the Arizona State saloon, noble sir," she said.

Louise smiled. No longer was she surprised or shocked at anything Sue said or did. Then Louise held out her arm and allowed Terry to take it. The scene had an element of humor to Louise, more so when she saw herself reflected in a window. It seemed strange that she should be walking down the street on a young gentleman's arm while dressed in a pair of jeans. She almost giggled but held it down for she saw how the giggle might sound and wanted nothing to spoil her friendship with the Ortega family, most especially with Terry.

Sue almost reached a table in the empty saloon when she stopped and pointed to the floor, looking at Eddy Last who stood behind the bar.

"What happened, Uncle Eddy?" she asked.

Louise looked down, seeing the patch of stained sawdust, a dull rusty-colored stain which she recognized.

"Fernandez," Last replied.

"Fernandez!" barked Terry. "Who did he kill?"

"He didn't. Got to riding Biscuits, trying to start a fight. Then Dusty Fog cut in and when the smoke cleared, ole Fernandez just hadn't made it at all. Then Manuel, him who was Fernandez's right bower, he tried to do it with a knife from the door. Which same Mark Counter coppered and they buries Manuel with Fernandez comes this afternoon."

"Dusty Fog?" Sue asked then looked toward Red. "I've heard tell of him. He hails from the Rio Hondo and pulls his guns like you pull your'n, Red."

"Nope," Red replied. "Cousin Dusty uses the cross-draw and I get mine out Cavalry twist-hand. Difference being Dusty could roll and light a smoke then still lick me to the shot."

"He's that fast?" Sue inquired.

"He's so fast the rest look slow."

The party sat eating their breakfast when the batwing doors opened to admit Dusty Fog and Mark Counter. For a moment Sue suspected a joke when Red whispered the small man's identity. Then she studied his dress, the way his guns hung, the general air of quiet competence about him and read him for what he really was. Sue knew a tophand when she saw one, she also knew a good man with his guns. Small or taller than a cottonwood, this Texan was Dusty Fog.

"This's Terry and Sue Ortega," Louise introduced, watching Dusty's and Mark's faces as she spoke.

If she hoped the words would cause a stir she received a disappointment for not by as much as a flicker of their eyes did Mark or Dusty show the names meant anything to them. They extended their hands to the Ortegas, then Mark glanced at the girls and asked:

"You been fighting?"

"Nope," Sue replied heatedly. "This's the latest fashion in the East."

More people began to arrive at the saloon and clearly the no ladies rule no longer applied, being waived as when the court held session or a meeting for the mutual good of the county formed. Women came into the saloon with their husbands, all wore their best clothes and an air of expectancy seemed to glow around them. A holiday spirit was abroad, laughter and chatter attesting to the general good feelings of the people as they moved about the room.

"It looks like you'll get your own way at last, Sue, Terry," a woman called as she passed the table.

"I always do," Sue answered.

People crowded into the saloon. The cowhands returned from giving their horses an unusually careful grooming and paying equally careful attention to their personal appearance. The town barber had been open all night; the owner of the store had long since sold out of his meager stock of shirts, trousers, hats and bandannas. No cowhand wished to appear before the ladies of the wagon train unless he looked his best and the extra effort would be worth while.

The citizens of the town, not that they were many in number, augmented by the ranch crews, crowded into the saloon. Outside the street held lines of buggies, horses and even the chuck wagons, for nobody wished to miss going out and meeting their new neighbors.

Biscuits Randle's appearance called for some jeers and comment among the cowhands for he sported a clean white shirt and a neatly fastened string tie. He halted at the Ortega table and grinned down at them.

"Are you coming with us, Biscuits?" Sue inquired. "Somebody might rob the bank while you're away."

"I ain't got no money in it, even if we had one to have it in," Biscuits replied. "Like you and Mark to take on as special deputies, Cap'n Fog. Times are like to get hectic and I'll need some help to keep the boys in control."

"Be pleased to," Dusty answered, holding out his hand to take the badge Biscuits offered.

"Let's take you around and get acquainted, Louise," Sue whispered. "I'm getting 'who is she?' looks from all our friends."

The girls left the table and Terry rose to join the ranch owners at the bar. Red rolled a smoke which his cousin extracted from his fingers. "Terry's not the one," Red drawled, offering Mark his makings and growling he was damned if he'd roll them as well as buy the tobacco and papers.

"Figured that from what we heard last night and what we've just seen," Dusty replied. "That's a nice gal you've got there, Cousin Red."

A flush of color came to Red's cheeks and Mark grinned. "I admire your taste for the first time, Red boy. I can't say much for hers though."

"Shucks, you'll be making folks think there's something between Miss Ortega and me," Red growled.

"Give it time and there's likely to be something," Mark chuckled, then held up his hand as he saw the angry glint coming into Red's eyes. "Hold hard now, hitting a special deputy town marshal's plumb likely to land you in jail."

"One of these days—" warned Red, leaving the rest of the threat hanging over Mark's head. "I'd say we should know this big *hombre* who just came in."

Dusty had seen the man and reached the same conclusion slightly ahead of Red. The tall man who crossed the floor bore a striking family resemblance to Miss Considine. His appearance was striking, almost as tall as Mark and broad although there was an air of well-padded luxury about him which no hard-worked cowhand could show. He wore a buckskin coat, white shirt with string tie, Eastern-style riding breeches and boots. He did not show any sign of a gun anywhere about him, not even to Dusty's keen and practiced eyes. Hat in hand the tall man went by the Texans and joined the ranchers at the bar to which Terry called Dusty, Mark and Red a few moments later.

"My sister is with the train," the tall man told Dusty after being introduced. "I hope she made the trip with no trouble."

"Lost all but two drivers, but she's all right," Dusty answered.

Considine then turned the conversation to the siting of the town. His conversation was of a high standard. He never talked down to the others, treated them as equals while still maintaining his well-educated superiority in view for all to see and respect. A smooth operator, Dusty guessed, a man who could stand some watching in anything he laid his hand to.

A man in range clothes entered the saloon. Dusty would not have noticed him among the crowd had Considine not given an almost imperceptible shake of his head and motioned toward Dusty with his hand. The man turned but not before Dusty got a good look at him. He appeared to be an ordinary cowhand, his clothes no different in quality or line from the man who worked at the local spreads. That he wore a gun meant nothing, so did every man in the room. It hung right for a fairly fast draw but did not have the appearance of being a real fast man's rig. The man's face caught Dusty's eye, somehow it looked familiar although he could not place it. The man did not stay. He turned and walked from the saloon once more and Dusty could have sworn a look of relief came to Considine's face when the batwing doors closed hiding the man from sight.

Dusty opened his mouth to tell Mark to follow the man but did not get a chance for Eddy pounded on the bar top.

"All right, folks," he yelled. "We're all here. Let's get out and meet our new neighbors."

The last two from the room were Louise Raines and Terry Ortega. She felt his arm crush hers and looked into his eyes. Louise felt happy. The wagon train would be welcome here in Backsight and she guessed she was more than welcome to the man called Terry Ortega.

CHAPTER ELEVEN

Dance Night in Backsight

THE Ysabel Kid and Colonel Raines watched the wagons streaming down the slope below the V-shaped gap in the hills. Throughout the train a feeling of excitement and expectancy prevailed, growing more and more plain with each turn of the wheels. Their new home lay ahead, so close after the long miles it almost passed beyond belief that nightfall would find them camped at Backsight ready to lay out their homes the following day.

"There's timber in plenty for the cutting up here in the hills, Colonel," remarked the Kid. "And you'll likely not find yourself short of hands to help with the house raising."

"Good," Raines replied distantly. "I was thinking about Louise. I hope she's all right. She should never have ridden ahead of us."

The Kid did not think it prudent at this point to mention he knew of the girl's departure. "She won't take no hurt. That girl's packed with good sense. I'd trust her to do anything she set out to do."

Raines looked at the Kid, a suspicion forming. To distract unwanted attention, the Kid pointedly stared ahead of them, drawing Raines' gaze after his own and effectively taking the Colonel's mind from his suspicions. Raines let out an angry grunt, reaching down for the field glasses he carried in his saddle pouch as he did so.

"Riders! A fair bunch of them and we let them get this close without seeing them!" he snapped. "It might be trouble."

"No trouble, Colonel," the Kid answered. "I've had them spotted for the last couple of mile or so. Dusty and Mark's up at the point with Louise, Red and a man 'n' gal I don't know."

Raines did not speak for a moment. He focused the glasses and was willing to admit the Kid possessed tolerably keen eyes. Raines could barely make out the riders with the naked eye yet the Kid not only saw but recognized them.

"What do you make of them?" asked Raines, although he could guess.

"Likely a welcoming party. Get them last wagons moving and on to the flat, Colonel. Then warn the drivers there's likely to be some whooping and hollering in the near future."

By the time the last wagon reached the level ground all the people of the train could tell something was in the air. They saw the approaching riders and buggies, knowing no trouble was on hand. A man did not come looking for trouble dressed in his best clothes and bringing his womenfolk along. Besides, Captain Fog rode at head of the approaching party so they could not be enemies.

Any slight doubt held became dispelled when the other party came to a halt. Hands and hats waved in a friendly manner. Louise sprang down from her horse, caught Terry by his hand almost before his feet hit the ground beside her. She ran to meet her father, smiling and crying at the same time. Raines dismounted, caught the girl in his arms. Then people were milling around, cheering, pointing and mingling with the citizens of Backsight County who advanced, hands held out to greet the newcomers with typical Western friendliness.

Eddy Last drew his revolver, fired a shot into the air to attract attention, aided by one of his famous bellows.

"Colonel Raines, ladies and gentlemen!" he yelled when partial silence fell. "On behalf of your neighbors of Backsight County, I greet you."

"Thank you, sir, thank you, " Raines replied. "On behalf of my fellow travelers, I thank you for this warm and inspiring welcome. I hope we will live up to the standard of friendship and hospitality this greeting brings to us. This is no time for speech making but I wish to thank Captain Fog, the Ysabel Kid, Mark Counter and Red Blaze for their help, without which we would undoubtedly never have arrived at all."

The thunderous cheers which rose repaid Dusty and his friends for the work and risks they gave and took bringing the train from Hammerlock. They'd done a good job, the train was at Backsight and the town could be built—unless the mysterious trouble causer still aimed to make trouble. Once the man behind the trouble was found they would be finished and could head back to Texas where most likely some other work awaited them.

The wagon train remained where it came to a halt for everyone was busy getting to know their new neighbors. The girls of the train eyed the cowhands with interest and speculated how they could form an acquaintance while the young men of the train and the ladies of Backsight studied each other and hoped to get to know each other better.

Miss Considine and her brother rode up to Raines as he stood talking with Last and the ranch owners.

"Colonel," she said, "My brother and I would like to suggest we hold a grand ball tonight in town to celebrate our arrival."

"It'll be expected," Considine went on. "You all need a chance to relax and the wagons will be safe enough if you form a circle by the stream near town."

Raines frowned, glancing around for Dusty's permission. The ranchers all gave their eager and vocal agreement to Considine's idea. So did such members of the train who heard. The news bounced from mouth to mouth and all seemed excited, eager at the prospect of the dance. Dusty came to Raines' side but could see there was no way of stopping the dance even if he wished to.

"All right, have your dance," he drawled. "But let's get rolling and make the circle first."

The wagons rolled soon after, surrounded by laughing riders while many of the women shared buggies with the ranchers' wives, all talking eagerly. Offers of help came from every hand.

Dusty rode ahead of the others, allowing Red and Louise to break the news to Raines that the young man who rode with them was Terry Ortega. He heard the Colonel's angry growl die away and knew Louise must have acted fast to prevent a scene. Dusty gave no thought to this, his mind was working fast as he thought of the dance. There would be no question of guarding the train, for every man, after the long trail, had set his mind on attending the dance.

Bringing the horse around Dusty rode back to the others and caught Terry's eye. The young rancher rode toward Dusty, falling in alongside the big paint.

"Your boys handle their guns?" he asked.

"Sure, not up to your or Mark's class though."

"Reckon they'd do something for me, happen it meant missing most of the dance?" Dusty went on.

"Reckon they—"

"Like I was saying," Dusty interrupted. "Cousin Red's got money saved, could make the right gal a good wife— howdy, Miss Considine, this here's Terry Ortega."

Miss Considine nodded her head, then rode by, her brother at her side. They left the train behind, making good time across the range toward the town.

"What's all that about?" Terry inquired, throwing a glance to where a grinning Duke rode by Louise, talking and pointing toward his boss. Terry could guess what Duke was telling Louise and wanted to get back in a hurry.

"I need some boys to help me guard the train tonight. The folks from the train are out, they'll want to be in on the dance and I don't know anybody I'd rather trust than you and your boys."

"They'll be on hand for you," Terry promised. "What do you reckon might happen?"

"I couldn't say. Not unless Jesse James comes out from Clay County. He robs trains they tell me."

Terry snorted. "I'm not sure I'd want my lil sister to marry into a family that tells tired jokes like that. Do you think Considine's behind this, shutting me up like you did when you saw them coming toward us."

"I don't think anything, except I want to make sure that only me and your boys know we'll be out there. I've an idea that'll get us away happen your spread's got a hoss they allow can run."

Dusty knew this to be more than likely. Almost every ranch owned one horse on which the crew would be willing to bet money in a horse race. Quickly Dusty told the young rancher his idea and Terry swore his men not only could carry it out but would show the Texans how such matters were done in Arizona Territory.

"Now I'm getting back to Louise afore young Duke busts up my ch—well, before he spoils—"

"You'd better go. I hate to see a man trying to make up something he doesn't need to make up."

Turning his horse Terry headed toward the main body. Duke saw his boss coming, raised his hat hurriedly to Louise, turned and bumped into Sue who gave him a sweet smile.

"Now won't Terry raise lumps on your pointed lil head when I tell him what you just told Louise," she said. "Save me doing it, pie-thief."

Duke set the spurs to his horse and lit out with all speed. Terry gave a wild yell and his crew saw Duke in full flight so left their duties to give chase. Dusty saw his chance, he gave a Texas cattle yell which sent Mark and the Kid in hot pursuit, followed by Red.

"Come on, Terry!" Dusty yelled. "Lend a hand with him."

The chase took all the men out of sight of the train and in a hollow Duke heard hooves thunder behind him. He turned and saw the two huge stallions bearing down on him, saw the futility of trying to escape for his go-to-town horse, good as it was, could not outrun Red's claybank and Mark's bloodbay. He was grabbed by his arms, lifted from his saddle and carried between the two riders to be dropped into a thorny bush. Duke's howls rose loud as he emerged from the bush to find the other riders waiting for him.

"Do we chap him, Terry?" grinned Tombstone.

"Naw, toss him in a blanket," whooped Red.

"Afore you start I'd like to tell you something," Terry replied. "Or rather, Dusty would."

Dusty spoke quietly. He saw the look of disappointment which came and then left the faces of the men. All saw the seriousness of the situation; they also saw a chance to have some fun and excitement so gave their willing agreement to Dusty's plan. They might miss the dance but they sure would have something to tell the folks of the train happen Dusty called the play right and their guarding became necessary.

The dance started just after nightfall, a scratch orchestra of anyone who could play an instrument and volunteered to help out supplied the music which, if not having the concerted flow of long rehearsal was loud and the audience did not show discrimination, being on hand to enjoy themselves.

Louise and Sue came with Red and Terry. Sue wore her best dress but felt a little piqued for Red retained his range clothes. During the first dance she saw the Lazy O crew and the Texans gathered in a corner. They were rowdy and gave every sign of hard drinking during the afternoon, for none could have reached their present stage of apparent inebriation since the dance started. She frowned as she watched. Like most cowhands her crew drank when in town. She knew they drank, knew also they did not become fighting drunk but hoped they would at least keep sober until the dance was well under way. That Dusty, Mark and the

Kid seemed to be drunk too came as a surprise to her, for they'd been with the Raines family most of the afternoon and not in a saloon.

"Put your money where your mouth is!"

Tombstone's bellow rang out over the sound of the music. Sue pulled away from Red, crossing the room with a hot flush of anger on her face. She saw Dusty haul some money from his pocket and in a drink-slurred voice reply:

"Here she is. Now let's see your hoss run."

"What's all this?" Sue snapped, forcing her way between the men.

Duke teetered on his heels and grinned. "We aims to show these lippy Texans a few lil things, Sue gal."

"But—but—"

Sue's angry splutter ended as the men went by her, making for the door. She could hardly believe her eyes as she watched Red and Terry go with the others. For a moment she stood with clenched fists, hearing the rapidly departing hooves and wild drunken cowhand yells fading as the men rode from town. Then a sudden suspicion hit her, for Sue knew her ranch crew.

"Something smells," she muttered to herself, a habit she gained from spending much time alone.

"May I take you on the floor for the next dance set, Miss Ortega?" Raines asked, following Dusty's orders to keep everything going in a normal manner.

Sue allowed herself to be led into a dance set but she could not shake the thought of something being wrong from her mind. "There's something dead wrong—" she began.

"Let's take the attention of the others from your brother and his crew's indiscretion, shall we?" Raines replied, sweeping the girl into the steps called from the bandstand.

Considine and his sister were by the side of the room watching everything. They joined in none of the dances and after a few moments the man who attracted Dusty's attention earlier entered the room, whispered to them and left. The big man rose to his feet, crossed the room to halt by Raines.

"How about asking Amelia to sing, Colonel?" he asked.

"I'd love to hear her again but it wouldn't look right for me to be pushing her onto the bandstand."

Raines nodded in agreement. The woman sang very well; she would make a pleasant entertainment for the people who appeared to be flagging from the earlier dances. So crossing the room Raines bowed to Miss Considine and after a few moments she agreed to sing.

Sue stood away from the other women, a puzzled frown on her face which did not lift when she saw Biscuits Randle paying very obvious attention to the woman Louise introduced as Maisie Simons. She liked Maisie on the short meeting they had and thought of how Biscuits was noted as a very good cook. The law enforcement duties of Backsight did not take up so much of his time that he would be unable to lend Maisie any hand she needed. Then Sue shook the thought from her head. That Dusty Fog and his cousin Red Blaze were going to need to do some tall explaining the next time they met up with Miss Sue Ortega. That she was certain sure of.

The cowhands kept up their drunken whooping and yelling for some way out of town, although the party had lost a member before they went half a mile. The Kid came up on his stallion, a broad grin playing on his face.

"He's not following us now," he remarked.

"Who was he?" Dusty asked, having let the Kid stay back to see if they were followed by suspicious people.

"I never saw a riding style like his afore, although I'm near to sure I know him from some place," drawled the Kid. "Could have caught him and likely made talk but you said I should let him go back to town."

"You reckon there'll be a try at the train?" Terry asked.

"It's the last chance to stop the folks meeting their contract on time," Dusty replied. "It'll be tonight or not at all."

"I'll fix your wagon but good, Cap'n Fog, if they don't come." Duke warned from the bunch of riders. "I'd just got me to know a sweet red-haired gal this afternoon and she don't look the sort to take to me drinking and whooping it up with the likes of you."

"Happen they come early enough you'll get to have a dance with her," Mark answered. "Happen that whiskery ole goat don't get us lost on the way to the train."

Tombstone gave a gritty growl which might have meant anything. To avoid suspicion Dusty insisted they go toward the Lazy O even though this took them away from the train circle. Tombstone was promoted to guide with orders to get them to the train and his knowledge of the lay of the land stood him well now.

Dropping from his saddle at the first sight of the train through the darkness, the Kid went forward. He had gone only ten minutes when his horse started to move forward in answer to his whistle.

"Dismount," Dusty barked. "Andy, take the hosses back there a good piece. Don't come in until I yell for you."

"I'll do that, Cap'n," growled the cowhand called Andy.

The wagons lay in darkness and Dusty set his men out so they could cover the entire area. Dusty, the Kid and Terry knelt by the side of the wagon with their guns in their hand, even the Kid preferring his old Dragoon to the Winchester in a situation of this nature.

Mark knelt by the side of a wagon with Duke at his side. To a young man of Duke's exuberant temperament, this waiting soon palled. He wriggled uncomfortably a couple of times then hissed:

"I hope they comes soon. Say, that lil red-haired gal, she stood about so high," he made signs in the dark. "And she surely looks—"

"Get mum and watch what you're doing," growled Mark. "That gal can't know what she's letting herself in for."

"I'll have you know I was much sought after in parts," Duke whispered back. "They used bloodhounds one time."

"Trust me to draw a pard like you."

"Don't worry none. I'll protect you."

The Kid touched Dusty's arm and whispered, "They're coming. Fair bunch of them. Moving nicer than I thought white men could."

Almost a minute ticked by before Dusty could hear anything. By that time he could also make out the dark shapes moving toward the wagons.

"Hold it there!"

Dusty's challenge floated from the darkness and he moved to one side even as he spoke. The precaution paid off. From the dark bunch of men came a sudden scuffle which saw them separate. A shot crashed loud, the flame lanced toward the wagons and a bullet struck wood.

Dusty threw a shot in echo, aiming at the gun-flash. Lead struck something but that something was not flesh. Instead a dull booming noise sounded, liquid splashed and there came a dull thud as something hit the ground. Dusty knew what he had hit, knew it and felt anger.

The Kid's old Dragoon loomed out then he hissed, "They're moving all round us. Likely allow there's a couple of guards."

"Likely learn different," Dusty answered.

Red and one of the middle-aged cowhands crouched side by side listening to the rapid crash of shots. Then Red grunted and lined his right hand Colt on a dark shape which crawled even closer. The gun barked and the shape lurched, then went limp.

"That Cap'n Fog was sure on to their game," whispered the other man, firing and hearing a sound similar to that which attracted Dusty at the front, although the cowhand gave no thought to it.

Mark and Duke found themselves engaged by two dark shapes who threw shots from the blackness. From all Mark saw he knew Duke would make a good fighting man when he learned prudence. A shot hissed over their heads, Mark fired at the flame and they heard a man scream, then a thrashing sound in the grass.

"Yahoo!" Duke whooped wildly. "You got him, Mark. Hear hi—"

From the sound of the thrashing grass came a spurt of flame and the crash of a shot. Duke gave a gasp of pain and went down. The man in the grass must have taken his aim on the sound, then made his move.

Mark was before the boy, crouching, cold anger on his face as he watched two dark shapes rise from the ground. Mark threw three shots, sending them in an arc which took both shapes. One screamed, spun around and fell, this time the grass thrashing was no trick. The second man flung himself to one side rolling for safety, sure that Duke had played them at their own game. Holstering his Colts, Mark bent over Duke, feeling for the wound. It was in his chest but the boy still breathed and needed help as soon as it could be brought to him.

Red fired two shots at the shapes which lay outside the circle. By his side the cowhand threw a bullet. Then Red heard a thud, a half cry and felt the cowhand kick his leg. He turned and not a moment too soon. A figure hurled from beside the still shape of the cowhand, something glinted dully and Red felt as if a burning brand ran down his arm. The Colt fell from his right hand but the unwounded left came up, slamming the barrel of his Colt against the jaw of the knife-wielding shape even as it came at him. A heavy shape smashed into Red; that and the pain of his ripped-open arm sending him flat on his back.

"Kid!" he roared and his left hand caught the knife-wrist once more but he knew he could not handle the strength of his attacker.

The Ysabel Kid was already on his way. He'd heard the noise and Red's yell brought him forward in a rush. The Dragoon went back into leather; this matter called for Mr. James Bowie's brainchild. The man kneeling astride Red did not even know the Kid was on him and never did. The Kid's left hand shot out, gripped hair, dragged back the head, then the right brought around the knife. Sharper than many a barber's razor the great blade ripped and sunk into the man's bared throat until it touched bone. The scalp yell of a Comanche split the air and the Kid flung the twitching body to one side.

"How bad is it, Red?" growled the Kid but there was concern in his voice.

"Hurts like hell," replied Red. "They got this boy without

a chance. Show them how to do it, Lon!"

The Kid's reply was a Comanche deep snarl. His gunbelt slid from his waist, then his boots were kicked off and Red suddenly found himself alone with the two bodies. The Kid was gone like a shadow. That had been an Indian he killed and the Indian never drew breath who could teach a Comanche anything about fighting in the night.

Through the blackness inched the Kid. He was not white now, the blood of Long Walker, the old man chief of the Dog Soldier lodge, pounded in his veins. He was out to kill. to make those dark shapes wish they'd never set eyes on the Raines wagon train. In his hand the bowie knife weighed heavy and was sticky even to his hand. He took a second to wipe the blood from the hilt and his palm. This was not the time for the hilt to slip through being slick with blood.

A man lay behind a bush firing at the train. The Kid inched forward, aiming at the gun flashes. His knife rose, fell, sinking into flesh, into the place where it would do most good. The man's body arched, his gun fell from his hand, but he never made a sound. The Kid turned to move when a thought struck him. His hand went to the body of his victim, feeling at the clothing.

"Mexicans!"

It was a thought, not a word. This man was a Mexican for sure; likely the others hailed from south of the border too.

Suddenly a man materialized at the Kid's side. He would have taken most men by surprise but not the Kid at such a moment. His coming had been silent yet the Kid was aware of him and full ready to deal with him.

"Pedro?" hissed the man.

"Sí!"

The man appeared to be fooled, then another voice from one side called in Spanish, "Who is that?"

The man half turned at the words, then he spun back yelling "Pedro! One of the—agh!"

It was full half a second too late. The Kid's knife ripped home, laying the man's belly open with the ease of a Cavalry saber. He felt the hot rush of air from the man's stomach and blood spurted out on to his shirt. The Kid went in fast, his hands catching the man and using him as a shield. Lead struck the body thrown by Pedro, but did not come through. The Kid hurled the body to one side, going the other way himself in a rolling dive which carried him to cover. He saw a man in front moving toward him and came up with his knife ripping home. The man screamed, the hideous scream of one in mortal agony and from the train came three bullets, one of which stirred the Kid's hair in passing.

"Dang goat," he thought as he went into cover and glided back toward the train once more. "I'm sure glad that wasn't either Dusty or Mark shooting."

In the dance Sue and the others heard the first shots but ignored them for the cowhands often played such a trick. Sue laughed as Louise asked if they should investigate.

"That's just what the boys want us to do," she replied but the smile died an uneasy death. The shooting continued, lasting longer than any cowhand who had to buy his own powder and lead would take for a mere joke. "That's from the wagons! Jim, Major Leyland, get some of the boys out there and pronto!"

The men made a rush for the door and Sue caught Raines' arm as he went after them. "What's it all about, Colonel?" she snapped.

"That's Captain Fog and your crew," Raines replied.

"Now I've got it. None of them smelled of liquor," Sue ejaculated grimly.

She darted to the bar and yelled for the loan of Last's ten gauge. The bartender handed it over for he knew Sue could handle the shotgun. She left the room hot on the heels of the men.

"They're going!" Dusty said to Terry Ortega. "Folks from the town are coming out with lights."

Red came over at that moment, holding his arm. "Caught a knife," he said in answer to Terry's query. "The Kid's gone out after them. I'm sorry, Terry, but they got Wade."

Before Terry could reply the Kid appeared between two of the wagons, coming in like a ghost. "I come in here, should be safer. One of your boys near on blew my head off."

The attackers made good their retreat, for there was no way Dusty and his party could follow. Dusty knew how dangerous it would be to roam around in the dark and so forbade the others to try it. He watched the lights approaching and called to ask if there were casualties.

"Duke's hit bad!" Mark yelled back. "We need a doctor here *pronto*!"

"Tombstone got his fool head nicked," called one of Terry's hands. "Came up a mite sharp and cracked it on the wagon bed."

"They were greasers," the Kid remarked. "Least those I found all were."

"Come ahead, gents!" Dusty called to the men who lit their way forward with lanterns and bar lamps.

The first to arrive was no gent but an irate and indignant lady. "Just what did you—" Sue began, then saw Red holding his arm. "Red, you're hurt!"

"I'm a dying cowboy and need loving care to keep me going," Red replied.

"I'll give you hell!"

"They got Wade and hit Duke bad," Dusty put in. "I'm sorry, Sue."

Sue felt the loss of Wade, a long standing friend, but she was a Western girl and practical at a time such as this. "The doctor can tend to Duke. I'll wind something round this scratch."

"Scratch!" Red wailed, knowing he could help Sue from brooding over the loss of her men.

"Scratch," Sue agreed, for the wound was little more than a long deep scratch, more messy and painful than serious. She hauled up her skirt, tore off a length of her petticoat and bound the wound in a workmanlike manner.

The other men gathered around and Dusty snapped orders

to them to make sure none of the gang remained close by. Then he rose and left the circle with Mark and the Kid to check their victims.

"Greasers every one," growled the Kid. "Pity we couldn't take any of them alive. They'd've talked plenty."

More men came up, Dusty saw the big shape of the land agent among them. His eyes went to the man's trousers as they showed in the light of a lantern. On the left leg Dusty saw a stain or wet-looking patch. However, before he could speak to Considine, Dusty heard Mark call.

"Found this, Dusty!"

Mark carried something forward; it was a large metal drum with a handle on top and one side burst by a bullet. Dusty did not need to ask what the drum contained for he knew a kerosene can when he saw it.

"Now we know what they aimed to do," he remarked. "Any of you folks know the Mexicans?"

"Two of them stood by Fernandez last night," Mark replied. "Could be their way of getting back at us."

"Get back to the train," Dusty drawled. "There's nothing we can do here."

In the circle Dusty's first action was to go where the doctor, with the light of lanterns, fought to save Duke's life. Sue looked toward Dusty and nodded reassuringly.

"He's got a fighting chance," she said. "Which same's all Duke ever asked for."

"I shouldn't have brought your crew—"

"Dusty Fog," Sue snapped. "I'm maybe not a smart gal, but I'm no fool and Red's kin better know that. You took our boys because you needed men you could rely on. They took their chances. I'll mourn for Wade and maybe Duke, but I'd hate to think they left you to stand here alone."

Red slipped his good arm around the girl's shoulders. "Will you marry me, Sue?" he whispered.

It was no time to ask such a question and the polite conventions of the time demanded a much longer acquaintance before asking it. Sue nodded her head without a second thought.

"As soon as your arm's better."

Dusty heard the proposal and its acceptance as he walked away. Sue could not have found a better man and Red would have a girl to be proud of, although hell only knew what Uncle Devil would say when he heard.

Colonel Raines waited for Dusty, standing clear of the others. The small Texan came straight to the point. "Who was missing from the dance, Colonel?"

"It's hard to say. Considine was there listening to his sister a short time before the shooting. I assume he was, as I got tangled in a discussion and couldn't watch him. The only other one who was missing, or who I noticed missing was Mrs. Simons."

"You sure about it, Colonel?" snapped Dusty.

"Near enough," Raines answered. "I remembered what you told me and looked especially for her. I asked Biscuits where she was, him having been pretty close to her all night. Allowed she'd left for the ladies' room just when the shooting started and hadn't come back."

Randle came up at that moment. His face was blank as he looked at Dusty.

"I thought I rated some trust, Cap'n."

"You did, but happen I told you, I'd've had to persuade you to stay behind and you're a man who'd take some persuading. It looked more natural with you not knowing about the shooting," Dusty replied. "Let's get back to town and I'll tell you what I know."

Mark and the Kid stayed behind with Lourde's men to clear up around the circle. The dance was called off when word got around and soon people were all in their beds. Dusty did not sleep that night, nor did Biscuits Randle, who learned all the small Texan knew but could shed no light on the possible trouble-causer.

Dawn came and Biscuits cooked up a meal for the Texans. They sat around the stove in the jail while outside the people of the town woke to another day. The office door burst open and a man entered.

"Cap'n Fog," he said. "I've just found Bull Gantry laid

out behind the civic pound."

"Reckon Gantry can tend to his drinking without me," Dusty replied.

"He's not drunk. He's dead. Shot in the head!"

Dusty and the others hurried out and among the bushes behind the corral looked at Bull Gantry's body. Dusty bent to examine the hole in his temple and came up to his feet, his face cold and hard.

"The thirty-six again," he said gently but there was no gentleness in his tone. "Where at's Sue and Louise?"

"With young Duke, been sat up with him," Mark replied.

"Let's get them. I'll need their help."

"What're you going to do, Dusty?" asked Randle.

"What I should have done a long time back. See Mrs. Simons and get some answers to a few puzzling questions."

CHAPTER TWELVE

Maisie Simons' Explanation

"BETTER go and get some rest, dear."

Louise spoke gently to Sue. The Western girl sat on a chair by the bed in which Duke lay, face pallid and chest hardly moving, so shallow was his breathing.

"Not yet," Sue replied quietly.

Louise laid her hand on Sue's shoulder and squeezed it gently. The ranch girl remained as she'd sat all night since Duke had been brought to the room in her house. Louise did not know how she might help and stayed by Sue, earning the other girl's undying friendship by so doing.

Duke's eyes opened, they were pain-wracked and yet when they rested on the two girls a bit of his old grin fought its way to his lips. "Man, two angels already to hand," he gasped weakly. "Won't that rile Tombstone 'n' Andy; they allowed I'd never get to it."

Sue bit down a sob of relief, her voice was hoarse as she replied. "Pie stealers don't go to heaven. Not any time. So you can just get up and quit your loafing."

"I ended where they said I would," Duke groaned. "I

165

knowed I should have listened to Tombstone."

"Are you all right, Duke?" Louise asked.

"Had I a lil red-haired gal about so high," Duke answered, feebly trying to move his hands, "I'd be all set."

The door opened and Dusty entered, followed by Mark, the train's preacher and the little red-haired gal about so high. She came forward, face pale but feet moving determinedly. The previous night after the fight Mark told the preacher of Duke's interest in the red-haired girl and she came willing to act as his nurse.

"Now I'll never get him well," sighed Sue but she gripped the girl's hand in her own and whispered, "Thanks, honey. Take care of him."

"I want you and Sue with me, Louise," Dusty snapped as the girls came to the side of the room.

"Why sure," Sue agreed. "Come on, Louise gal. This's no time to ask fool questions."

The two girls followed Dusty and Mark from the house. The Kid leaned by the picket fence, his rifle in his hand. "Quiet as the Staked Plain at noon," he said. "Nothing stirred no place."

"Let's go then," replied Dusty. "Keep behind us, girls, and be ready to hit the ground if I give the word."

"What's wrong, Dusty?" Louise gasped.

"Just do what he says, don't jaw," Sue answered, for Dusty did not speak.

Louise suddenly realized where they were heading. On the previous day, with the eagerly given aid of Biscuits and Eddy Last, Maisie Simons had erected a large tent. She declared her intention to open for business the following day and brought her gear to town. Dusty headed straight for the rear end of the tent where already the Chinese helpers prepared food.

Maisie sat at a small table at the end of the building and nodded a greeting as Dusty came toward her, followed by Mark and the girls, the Kid having stayed at the door watching the street outside.

"Good morning, Captain," Maisie greeted. "Can I get your party anything?"

"Why sure. I want that long-barreled Navy Colt, then for you to go with Louise and Sue and strip."

"Dusty!" Louise gasped, sounding shocked and angry.

"Very well," Maisie said, coming to her feet. "Come on, girls. We'll use my wagon for it."

"Just what in hell are we supposed to be looking for?" Sue inquired.

"A recent scar, likely to be small and any place but most likely on the left side of her body."

"I could explain it all, Captain," Maisie remarked. "But I'd better clear this for you first, then talk after."

Maisie and Louise started toward the door but Dusty drew his left hand Colt, passing it to Sue. "Keep it hidden but if she tries to pull a gun, or get her hands out of sight, use it."

Time passed and Sue returned. "Nary a scar, not new. She's got one that looks like it came from a knife and a couple which could have been made by teeth in a brawl but no new scars at all. What's it all about, Dusty? She allows to have something to tell you if you'll come into the wagon."

Dusty and Mark followed Sue to the wagon, the girl returning his Colt before they entered. Maisie finished buttoning her dress and waved her hand to the twelve-inch-barreled Navy Colt which lay on her trunk, holding down a wallet of a type Dusty recognized.

"I demand an explanation, Dusty!" Louise snapped. "You've made accusations or insinuations about Maisie ever since you met her. Now I want to know what this's all about."

"First off, Mrs. Simons, if that's your name," Dusty drawled, ignoring the girl, "I want some answers."

"I'm not sure I should answer them, or that you have the authority to ask," Maisie said coolly.

"Biscuits made Mark and I special deputies and we're still working for him ma'am," Dusty drawled. "Do we do it the easy way or use your Pinkerton's methods?"

Maisie smiled, her eyes going to the wallet. The other two girls stood back looking on. Sue caught Louise by the arm and held her, growling a warning not to interfere.

"All right, I work for the Pinkerton Agency. That's my identity wallet and inside it is a letter of instruction."

Dusty took up the Navy Colt, checked the cylinder and found it full loaded though not capped. He drove the barrel retainer out and lifted the barrel out of place, looking through.

"All right, it's not been fired recent," he said and assembled the gun once more. "Why did you leave the train and go into Hammerlock, that night we arrived?"

"Two reasons. To check up with one of our operatives who lives in Hammerlock, the other to follow a suspect."

"Now listen, Mrs. Simons," Dusty spoke quietly and grimly. "I know the way you Pinkertons work and I'm not having it here. I want to know everything and I mean everything, no holding back until you can contact your boss and have him come here with a flock of newspapermen to get stories of how he arrested the Considines when the local law was helpless."

"All right, Captain. I should have laid my cards on the table a long time ago. Lord, I'm sick of this life. Tired of doing the dirty work and letting Allen Pinkerton get the glory. Tired of being a saloon girl with men pawing over me and a jealous girl trying to knife me or scratch my eyes out. I've never been treated so decently as I was with the train. I've all the evidence and should be getting it up to Allen, even if there is a chance that the Considines slip through our fingers and spend all the money they've made before we take them. But I'm throwing it all in your lap, every bit of it. Then I'll send my resignation in—but I've got to have something in return."

"Name it," Dusty replied.

"I've got to stay Mrs. Simons. It's my real name. I want to stay on here as Maisie Simons who runs the café."

"None of us will say anything, Maisie," Louise put in.

"Won't likely be more than Louise who knows about it in town in a month or so," Sue agreed, then blushed, for she and Red intended to keep their wedding a secret until his arm was better.

"You've got a deal," Dusty said, putting the official seal of approval on the matter. "Talk ahead."

"Well you may or may not know that three other trains put up their money for this section of land," Maisie explained, sitting at the box and shoving her wallet toward Dusty. "Not one of the three arrived and all lost their deposit."

"The governor never mentioned that to father," Louise put in.

"He didn't know of it. From all the official records at Prescott, this section has never been offered for sale once."

Mark whistled. "That means somebody made a tolerable pile of money."

"Yes. The first party were contacted by a woman answering Miss Considine's description. They left Saint Jo, Missouri, and became so discouraged that they broke up and sold out in Kansas. The second were a religious group, one of the kind who hold everything other than breathing is sin. They hardly made the Kansas line before they'd been scared off by nightriders. The last bunch were German immigrants who put every cent they owned into coming out here." Maisie went on and a smile flickered to her lips. "You might not believe this but Allen Pinkerton's made all this investigation just because of those people. He's using every facility of the agency to break this ring and doesn't stand to make a cent out of it."

"I wouldn't give him credit for hauling his mother from under a runaway wagon unless there was money in it for him," Mark growled.

Maisie's smile held. Allen Pinkerton and his agency were not liked by any Southerner. Mark's view of Pinkerton was much the same as held by practically every man south of the Mason-Dixon line. She did not try to excuse her employer but carried on with her story.

"The other two groups were split up; they could produce no papers to show their deal. Neither could the Germans. On questioning, the Germans admitted the woman who made the deal kept all the papers, receipts, everything. We had nothing to go on until we heard of Colonel Raines coming west. Now this train was different, they'd the Governor's backing. We thought it would break up the Considine game but had a man watching Raines. Then word reached us that Miss Considine was in Nashville and Allen decided to put me on the train. I saved the three Chinese from some bad trouble with their tong and they came along as my bodyguards and to make my story about going west more likely."

"Did you know they aimed to kill Tom Blade?" Mark growled.

"If I had I'd've tried to stop it," Maisie replied, her voice a little angry. "Don't let your ideas of Pinkertons fool you. We're working for law and order, just the same as any law enforcement body that's run by the state, territory or federal government. I didn't know Tom was marked for murder and I could have taken Considine apart with my bare hands when I heard, but that wouldn't prove anything. I went into Hammerlock hoping to find her but I didn't see her at all. I saw Collins and recognized him from his description. He and Hooks Hammer led the gang who scared off two of the other trains. By the way, Hammer's in town."

"I haven't seen him," Dusty answered.

"You have, Captain, twice at least. He's shaved his beard off—"

"Got him now, the man who came into the saloon yesterday and got out when Considine wig-wagged to him."

"The idea of killing Tom's easy enough, god damn her cold-blooded heart," Maisie went on. "And believe me, Captain, she's the brains behind this business, not her brother. Tom died and if Collins forced the Colonel to take him on as scout, then they headed for the gap in the hills and the train would be stuck. Sure the deposit would be lost, but the land agent gets a percentage on sales and that would stop a complete loss on the trip. Governor Mansfield couldn't make an exception in his friend Colonel Raines' favor, not without raising a political storm. So, unless a fresh deposit could be gathered, payment and improvements as per contract made, the Colonel would have to give up his idea of building up Backsight and the Considine family be left to ruin other folks. If the Colonel had the money there would be another percentage slice which could start them up in some other small town."

"We threw that game out, I reckon," Dusty drawled.

"You and Collins. His play was to sit back until news spread that Tom was dead, then cut in and offer to take on as scout. But he was a drunken fool and went bullheaded at it."

"It was her Collins saw in town, must have told her what happened," Dusty put in. "She saw how scared he was and stuck around. Then when he was set to talk with us she shot him."

Louise looked from Maisie to Dusty, her face showing the horror she felt. It did not seem possible that two people could so calmly discuss murder. "Aren't you going to do something?" she gasped.

"Just as soon as we know everything," Dusty replied. "She's a smart woman, one wrong move and she's off the hook. After Hammerlock, Maisie, they tried to play it with the cards they held. The gap was still their bet until the Kid called it. Even with the Apache attack she tried. Tossed an arrow with the message outside your wagon. You'd've seen her only you pulled that fake faint. Why'd you do it?"

"I heard a man saying about the shooting I'd done, how good it was. So I knew an Eastern widow wouldn't be expected to handle a gun well and thought if I pulled a faint they'd think either it was one of my boys, or just luck that I made the hits. I tried to steer suspicion away and only piled more on me. What was the message?"

"Warning the Colonel to stay away from Backsight. On the back were marks left by someone writing on a sheet of paper which laid on the message, it had Terry Ortega's address on, like another the Colonel received."

"Which's how you came to blame Terry for it, Louise," Sue remarked. "I wondered why they picked on Terry?"

"I don't think they did in the first place," Dusty drawled. "I'm only guessing though and we'll likely never know for sure. What I reckon happened was that Considine wrote the first note on a sheet in his office, after he'd been writing to Terry and the address was just there. Miss Considine claimed to have sent a telegraph message to her brother to learn about Terry."

"There's no telegraph here," Sue pointed out.

"No, it was a slip she made, didn't expect us to get out here," agreed Dusty. "But we arrived and I reckon they were set to make their last try, burn out the wagons."

"Which you stopped," Maisie said.

"I thought a chance might be taken so got the guard out. Considine used Fernandez' gang for the raid; they'd likely take on to make some money before they lit out for the border," Dusty replied. "All the men we downed were Mexicans, except for the Yahqui Indian the Kid killed, but he was likely one of Fernandez' gang. A lot of these Mexicans have a Yahqui or two running with them if they can, scouts, sneak-in killers, torturers for the gang. I don't reckon Considine was using any of his own men on the raid."

"He hires Hammer and two more, they're with him at the office now," Maisie replied. "They weren't on the raid but stood back to give him an alibi. He was with the Mexicans."

"Can you prove it?" Mark inquired.

"Sure," agreed Maisie. "I can prove it. Last night I got friendly with Biscuits Randle—"

"Last night?" grinned Mark, for there was never a situation so grim that he couldn't see the humor of it. "Why ole Biscuits and Eddy Last were sniffing around you like hound-dawgs when a bitch's in season all yesterday afternoon."

To the amazement of the others Maisie blushed furiously. The truth was that the hard-bitten lady detective felt attracted to the big burly town marshal. Her tough exterior hid a woman's heart and Maisie's trip West softened the hard outer crust. For the first time in years Maisie lived with decent, ordinary people, instead of saloon workers of the lowest kind. She'd watched families living normal lives, husbands and wives sharing simple pleasures and Maisie yearned for such a life. The big lawman was not as smart as one of the Pinkerton men who had made attempts, not all unsuccessful, on Maisie's virtue, but he was rugged, clean, gentle and would stand by her if she gave him one ounce of encouragement.

"I only wanted to find out what sort of a lawman he is," she muttered, still blushing. "He might've been working with Considine and—"

"Why sure," chuckled Mark. "We believe you, Mrs. Simons, ma'am."

"I reckon we'd better get back to what we're here for," Dusty remarked. "I never had a harder job than stopping Biscuits raising lumps on my head when I said I wanted to question you, Maisie."

"He's a tolerable hard man to hold down," Mark agreed.

Maisie noticed the way Dusty used her name. She knew the meaning. Dusty accepted and trusted her. So she fought down the embarrassment and carried on:

"I was with Biscuits until I heard the first shot. You'd have passed for a drunk, Captain, but not many of the others. Guessed what it was and got out the back to see what I could learn. The land agent's office was locked but I know how to open a lock and I went in to search. I was still in there trying to open the safe when they came back. Just got into a cupboard at the side of the office as the Considines and their men came in. I could see through the keyhole of the cupboard, it's a big one built into the side of the wall, and hear all they said. Miss Considine was telling her brother just what she thought of him. She really laid into him. Then she told the men to go and fetch a new pair of pants from their house. After the door closed she started into her brother again. From what I could make out was that Bull Gantry had left the dance to tell you something and she fixed him."

"She fixed him all right," Dusty said gently. "I reckon Gantry wasn't all bad at that."

"He changed after the fight on top of the slope. I watched him; he liked you after that night when you saved the train," Masie replied. "Miss Considine said she left him in some bushes where he wouldn't likely be found too quick, cleared up her sign as she came away from him and got back to the Arizona State without being missed by the other women. Her brother wanted to quit, to run, but she just said it would be the surest way to bring suspicion down on them. 'Nobody can prove a thing, you fool,' I can hear her saying it now. 'We'll just have to cut our losses and find some other place to operate.' Lord, I've seen some cold-blooded ones but she beats them all."

"How'd he get out of the saloon without being noticed?" Mark inquired. "I thought the Colonel was watching him and Maisie?"

"He was; it made me rather uncomfortable. But Considine asked the Colonel to persuade his sister to sing, knowing everyone's attention would be on her. She really can sing. The Colonel did and while he was talking to her Considine slipped out. His men would swear he never left the room and nobody could prove he did, not for certain."

"Then we can't prove he was with the raid?" Dusty asked.

"We can prove it," Maisie replied. "I was set to jump them and take them to jail when the men came back. Miss Considine cleared them all out of the room while her brother changed his trousers, left the pair he wore at the dance over the back of a chair. So I waited until they left, locking the door. Came out and collected the pants, left the same way I got in, locking the door behind me. The pants are in my box. They're what will hang Considine and his sister."

Maisie lifted the lid of the box and lifted out a pair of trousers. She handed them to Dusty, indicating a stain on

the left leg. He lifted the trousers to his nose, the stench
of kerosene clung to them.

"I saw the stain last night," he remarked. "This's all we
want. Let's go, Mark."

"One thing, Maisie," Mark put in. "You said you were
set to jump them and hand them over to Biscuits last night.
That means you'd decided to throw in your resignation even
before you arrived."

"You might say that," Maisie replied. "It wouldn't do
Biscuits any harm to be known as the man responsible for
arresting the Considines and breaking their crooked game.
Of course I don't want him to be a lawman when—if—"

"We can guess what that 'when or if' means," drawled
Dusty.

"Where're you going, Dusty?" Louise asked, watching
the way the two men set their guns straight.

"To get the folks responsible for Tom's death and make
sure you folks can build your town and live here in safety."

The girl looked at Dusty's face. She could remember
seeing it set in those same grim lines before, as he stood
over the grave in which Tom Blade lay buried. Her eyes
went to Mark, the big blond man no longer smiled as his
powerful hands thumb-hooked into his belt.

"Can't you let the law handle it?" she gasped.

"We're the law in this town, Louise," Mark replied.
"All the law there is, not counting Biscuits and he'll be on
hand when we need him."

Sue's face was set in cold lines. "You mean they, the
Considines, caused Duke to be wounded and Wade getting
killed?"

"Sure," Dusty replied.

"Let me get the crew out to help you," she suggested.

"No thanks, gal," Dusty answered. "There's four of them
and four of us. It comes out better odds than a lawman
usually gets. You stay here. See she does, Louise. I
wouldn't want Cousin Red's gal getting hurt."

With that the two men walked from the tent. Sue's face

glowed with anger and she took a step forward but Louise caught her arm.

"Dusty gave me an order, Sue," she warned. "I'll stop you any way I can."

"You're both stopping here," Maisie put in. "Don't argue with me or I'll crack your heads together."

"Reckon you would at that," grinned Sue. "Louise and I could take you, if you didn't have something more important to do."

"I didn't think it showed."

Maisie opened a box of percussion caps as she spoke, taking the little brass cups and seating them on the nipples of the Navy Colt's chamber. She moved fast and there was no trembling to her fingers even though she knew she might be using the Colt very soon.

"Stay here, both of you," she ordered and went through the side entrance to the tent.

"What's Maisie going to do?" Louise asked.

"Help Dusty. Now sit down and make sure I don't leave this tent while I do the same for you."

Louise sat by Sue on the box. She felt a sudden cold fear, a premonition of what would soon be happening on the street. Louise hated the thought of more killing, blood had been shed to prevent their reaching Backsight. Tom Blade, the man called Collins, the people who died in the Apache attack, the Apaches themselves who fell, the Mexicans killed the previous night and Bull Gantry. They were all dead because the wagons came to Backsight. Louise wondered if the killings were worth it. Then she remembered the excited and delighted way the townspeople and the local ranch crews greeted their arrival. She remembered Terry's eager talk of a school, a church, a town fit for children to grow in. Did it balance with the lives lost in coming? Louise did not know; only time would tell.

Dusty walked to the center of the street with Mark at his left and the Kid by his right. The few people on the street watched them, the Westerners among them knowing what such a walk meant. The Texans used the gunman's sidewalk, the center of the street, that told eyes which knew that they were painted for war.

Biscuits came from his office, a ten gauge looking like a toy in his huge hand. He fell in to Mark's right asking, "Is Maisie all right?"

"Sure and in the clear," Dusty replied. "It's the Considines we want."

"They're in the office, got five men with them," the Kid drawled.

"Maisie said three," Mark drawled.

"Two are greasers, likely from the bunch last night," answered the Kid and stroked the butt of the rifle laying across his arm. "There'll be a hot time in the old town tonight."

Terry Ortega and Red Blaze came around a corner, halting on the side of the street and reading the signs. Each of them had an arm in a sling but Red's gunbelt rode around his waist and he could handle a Colt with his left hand.

"Trouble, Red," Terry said. "Do we—"

"Nope, we stay here," Red replied. "I reckon I know where they're going and we can cover this side."

Terry Ortega glanced across the street. "Then it's them after all."

"Looks that way," Red agreed.

They stood slightly below the land agent's office.

CHAPTER THIRTEEN

The End of the Chore

MISS CONSIDINE watched her brother searching the office and a look of disgust came to her face. She made an attractive figure in her white blouse and divided skirt but was less interested in her appearance than in the utility of the clothes in case a sudden departure became necessary.

"They must be here someplace," he said for the fifth time.

"They're not," she snorted, ignoring Hammer, the last of the bull-whackers, a gunman and the two Mexicans who stood by the wall of the office. "I told you to keep those trousers with you. If they fall into the wrong hands it'll be our end."

Considine looked at his sister. "They were on the chair at my desk last night. I'm sure of it."

"Then somebody broke in and took them. It's that damned Maisie Simons. I'm sure it is. She's no Eastern widow. She's a Pinkerton and she's got those trousers. So we'd best put some miles between us and Backsight. One thing's for sure, if she works for Pinkerton she'll wait for word from him before she gives the local law anything she knows."

With the instinct of a fish when the net closes around it, Miss Considine felt herself being drawn into a trap. The time for a hurried departure had come and she meant to leave while she could. The money made in their scheme lay in a Prescott bank and they could withdraw it before word reached the territorial capital, for Backsight had no telegraph. In the office safe enough money remained to ensure the loyalty of these five men until their services no longer remained necessary.

"Where're we going?" Considine asked.

"East," she answered, not wishing the men to know too much.

"Considine!" the voice came from the street. "Come out, we've got the place surrounded and you haven't a chance."

"It's Dusty Fog and the other two," Hammer gasped as he looked out of the window. "They've got Biscuits Randle with them."

Miss Considine's face was hard. The horses stood before the building ready and she knew the Texans did not have their mounts ready. Once on her big stallion she was game to take her chances in flight. More so when she would have a lead on the pursuit and knew this country.

"Get out and fight!" she ordered. "It's our only chance."

Considine pulled a revolver from the desk and headed for the door. His neck would be in a noose if taken alive, so would the necks of the two Mexicans. Hammer and the other gunmen did not have much to lose, but they did not realize it. To them arrest might only mean Yuma prison but they knew what a hellhole it was and preferred to fight rather then end up behind its grim walls.

Guns in hand, the men made for the door. Miss Considine slid open the desk and took out her Remington Beals Navy revolver. Crossing to the safe she took out the saddlepouch which contained the money. The revolver in her right hand gave her a feeling of security for it ended the lives of Cultus Collins and Bull Gantry. Both meant to give the game away to that small Texan, Dusty Fog, Collins through fear and Gantry because he admired the Rio Hondo gun wizard. She shot both with no more thought than she'd give to dressing in a morning. Now she needed the gun and swore to end the life of Dusty Fog if given a chance.

"Get out of it!" she ordered.

Considine kicked open the door and plunged through. This was his chance to show his sister that not only she had the guts in the family. He saw the men before him and started to raise the revolver as the others of the bunch followed him.

Dusty Fog did not expect this, the rush and attack. For all that he was ready, prepared to draw and shoot. His hands crossed, the matched Colts coming out and throwing lead into Considine even as the big man lifted his gun. Considine spun around like a child's top, smashed into the wall and slid down, his gun dropping from his lifeless hand.

Mark was second into action, even although the Kid and Biscuits only needed to bring their weapons from their arms. In a breath behind Dusty's shots the ivory-handled guns thundered and Hooks Hammer hunched forward, his Colt sending a shot into the wood of the sidewalk, cut down by Mark's .44 bullets.

The two Mexicans plunged out, shooting fast as they came. One bullet tore the Kid's hat from his head as flame blossomed from the barrel of his Winchester. Held hip high it was the old yellow boy's flatnosed Henry bullet that smashed into the Mexican's face and shattered the back of his head on its way out. The second Mexican tried to cut down on Dusty but was off balance. The others lay before him and he tried to get clear. The ten gauge in Biscuits' hands boomed and the nine buckshot charge scythed across the fancy charro shirt, laying a bloody swathe and piling him on to the floor.

The gunman was last out, diving over the falling bodies of the others, his revolver flaming. Fanning was never a matter for careful aim and skilled shooting and so it proved this time. He lit down rolling on the sidewalk, his gun's smoke partially hiding him from Dusty and the others. It did not hide him from Red Blaze who brought up his left-hand Colt shoulder high, sighted fast and threw a shot. The gunman screamed as lead caught him. The revolver pin-wheeled on his triggerfinger as his grip relaxed and he dropped forward yelling he was done.

The powder smoke started to blow away as startled faces came to the doors and windows of the buildings.

Then Miss Considine burst from the building with her revolver in one hand, the saddlebag in the other. The men hesitated, holding their fire for she was a woman. The brains behind the organization she might be but she was still a woman, and no Western man of Dusty's kind would willingly fire on a member of the opposite sex.

The same did not apply to Miss Considine. She fired as her feet hit the sidewalk and only that she slipped on the slick blood which spread over the wood saved Dusty. The bullet went astray, caught Biscuits in the leg and dropped him to the ground.

Maisie Simons came around the corner of the building, her long barrelled Navy Colt lining. She fired once and Miss Considine screamed. The bullet caught the big woman in the arm, her Remington fell to the sidewalk and she went to her knees with her left hand clawing for it. Maisie came forward, a hard look changed her usually pleasant face and she brought up the revolver then slashed it down. The barrel smashed on to the back of Miss Considine's neck even as the woman's hand closed on the Remington's butt. She sprawled forward, landing face down half off the sidewalk and apart from the spasmodic jerkings of her fingers lay perfectly still.

"That was for Tom Blade!" Maisie hissed.

Dusty and his men moved forward to disarm the Considine bunch. Hammer might live and Red's victim would be on his feet in a few weeks but the rest lay as dead as cold mutton. They took their chances, made their play and fell at the hands of the law.

Hearing a tearing sound Dusty turned and looked to

where Maisie knelt by Miss Considine. She'd dragged the big woman on to the street, rolled her on to her back and tore open the blouse. With angry hands Maisie ripped the woman's underskirt.

"There's your proof that she shot Collins, Captain Fog," she said, pointing to a small but deep and barely healed scar just under Miss Considine's breasts. "She didn't want the other women to see the knife scar and went downstream of them. I sneaked up·on her and saw she was bathing a new cut and guessed it was something she didn't want talking about. That's what you had the girls check me out for, I reckon."

Raines and several of the ranchers came up, a crowd following. Dusty turned to face them.

"All right, folks, it's all over," he said. "Keep back."

Raines with the ranchers came forward. They were the leading citizens of the community and had the right to investigate such an incident. Mark and the Kid left matters in Dusty's hands as they stepped forward and halted the rest of the crowd.

Maisie went to Biscuits who sat on the ground holding his leg. The .36 bullet had passed through missing the bone and blood pumped from the wound. "Let me fix it for you," she said gently.

"You take care of your prisoner, ma'am," Biscuits replied. "If I'd a wife, she'd handle the she-male prisoners for me."

"I reckon I might be able to do that for you," Maisie whispered. "Let's talk about it later."

Raines stood by Dusty, while on the street beyond, Terry and Red went to meet the girls as they came from Maisie's tent. The Colonel pointed down to the groaning woman as Miss Considine fought her way back to consciousness.

"It was her after all," he said.

"Sure, Colonel. All the time," Dusty replied. "It's the end of the chore for us. We'll be headed back to Texas as soon as the trial's over."

"You won't stay on here with us then?"

Dusty laughed. "And have Uncle Devil rolling up in his wheelchair to give us hell?" he asked. "I'd as soon not, thank you 'most to death. Lon, Mark and I'll be riding home as soon as we can and Red 'n' his missus'll follow as soon as they're Red and his missus. Which same won't be long at all."

WANTED:
Hard Drivin' Westerns From

J.T. Edson's famous "Floating Outfit"
adventure series are on every Western fan's
MOST WANTED list. Don't miss *any* of them!

___THE BAD BUNCH	05228-1/$1.95	
___CUCHILO	04836-5/$1.95	
___THE FAST GUN	04802-0/$1.95	
___.44 CALIBER MAN	04620-6/$1.75	
___FROM HIDE AND HORN	04621-4/$1.95	
___GO BACK TO HELL	05618-X/$1.95	
___GOODNIGHT'S DREAM	04633-8/$1.75	
___THE HALF BREED	04736-9/$1.95	
___HELL IN THE PALO DURO	05294-X/$1.95	
___THE HIDE AND TALLOW MEN	05069-6/$1.95	
___THE LAW OF THE GUN	05311-3/$1.95	
___THE QUEST FOR BOWIE'S BLADE	05654-6/$2.25	
___THE PEACEMAKERS	05529-9/$1.95	
___THE TROUBLE BUSTERS	05227-3/$1.95	

Berkley Book Mailing Service
P.O. Box 690
Rockville Centre. NY 11570

Please send me the above titles. I am enclosing $_____
(Please add 50¢ per copy to cover postage and handling). Send check or money
order—no cash or C.O.D.'s. Allow six weeks for delivery.

NAME_____

ADDRESS_____

CITY_____STATE/ZIP_____

104 M

More shoot-'em-up action from

J.T. Edson

___THE HOODED RIDERS	04622-2/$1.75
___A HORSE CALLED MOGOLLON	04632-X/$1.75
___McGRAW'S INHERITANCE	05073-4/ $1.95
___QUIET TOWN	04623-0/$1.95
___RANGELAND HERCULES	04626-5/$1.95
___SET TEXAS BACK ON HER FEET	04413-0/$1.75
___SIDEWINDER	05070-X/$1.95
___THE SOUTH WILL RISE AGAIN	04491-2/$1.75
___TO ARMS! TO ARMS, IN DIXIE!	04162-X/$1.75
___TRAIL BOSS	04624-9/$1.95
___TROUBLED RANGE	05071-8/$1.95
___WAGONS TO BACKSIGHT	05951-0/$2.25
___THE WILDCATS	04755-5/$1.95
___THE YSABEL KID	05067-X/$1.95
___A TOWN CALLED YELLOWDOG	04850-0/'$1.95
___THE RUSHERS	05638-4/$2.25

Berkley Book Mailing Service
P.O. Box 690
Rockville Centre, NY 11570

Please send me the above title. I am enclosing $_____
(Please add 50¢ per copy to cover postage and handling). Send check or money
order—no cash or C.O.D.'s. Allow six weeks for delivery.

NAME_____

ADDRESS_____

CITY_____ STATE/ZIP_____